Love's Eternal Legacy

Love's Eternal Legacy

A Novel
Based on Near-death
Experiences

Arvin S. Gibson

First Printing: July, 1998

International Standard Book Number:

0-88290-504-X

Horizon Publishers' Catalog and Order Number:

1955

Printed and distributed
in the United States of America by

& Distributors, Incorporated

Mailing Address:
P.O. Box 490
Bountiful, Utah 84011-0490

Street Address:
50 South 500 West
Bountiful, Utah 84010

Local Phone: (801) 295-9451
WATS (toll free): 1 (800) 453-0812
FAX: (801) 295-0196

E-mail: horizonp@burgoyne.com
Internet: http:// www.horizonpublishers.com

Dedicated to the memory of a marvelous lady,
Marguerite Gibson Gaisford,
who died at age 27.

Acknowledgments

This book would not exist save for the efforts and encouragement of many people. First among those is the marvelous lady, Carol Gibson, whom I somehow was wise enough to marry forty-four years ago in Berkeley, California. Carol continues to be my right arm. She assisted with the many interviews in the research for the two preceding books (*Glimpses of Eternity*, and *Echoes From Eternity*), and she offered helpful comments throughout *Love's Eternal Legacy*.

Duane Crowther has consistently encouraged and supported my work in the field of near-death experiences (NDEs). When I approached him with the first draft of a novel reflecting some of what I had learned during my research, he and his staff reviewed the manuscript and made very helpful suggestions. Two editors in particular, Ron Safsten and Lorin May, made very constructive comments. Among other suggestions that I subsequently incorporated into the text was the addition of the last three chapters in the book. As you read the story, consider what it would have been like without the last three chapters. I am sure you will agree that Duane Crowther, and his people at Horizon Publishers and Distributors, contributed much to the finished product.

Gary Gillum, who's unusual NDE is described in detail in *Glimpses of Eternity*, provided substantial insight in his Foreword for this book. I am grateful for Gary's substantial help in this effort and in the previous work.

Florence Susan Comish was gracious in providing the dramatic painting *Love's Eternal Legacy* that graces the jacket cover of this book. Susan has painted the pictures for the last three of my books, and the books are significantly enhanced by her talent.

Rose Mari Finter, as with my previous books, again labored to improve my grammar and writing style. Her careful attention to detail helped me avoid embarrassing mistakes.

Several people read a draft of the book and offered helpful comments. Included in that group are: Dr. Mark Taylor, Dr.

3

Philip Pluta, Dr. B. Grant Bishop, Mrs. Patricia Pexton, Mr. Ralph Mabey, Mrs. Leanne Mayo, Mr. Fred Beckett, Ms. Marcia Darché, Mr. Jeremy Masterson, and Mr. Sid Stephenson. I am grateful for their diligence and useful suggestions.

Virginia Matzek, the Associate Editor of the *California Monthly,* was helpful in providing current information about the University of California. Personnel at the St. George and Oakland Temple Visitors' Centers for The Church of Jesus Christ of Latter-day Saints provided necessary descriptions of the types of tours available at the centers.

The Utah Chapter of the International Association for Near-Death Studies (IANDS of Utah) was a fertile source of help. The officers of that group were supportive of my effort, and many of the experiences incorporated into the story-line of the book came from the local members of IANDS.

All of us doing research in the near-death field are indebted to those pioneers that initiated the research work and first brought it to the attention of the world. Foremost among the early research-ers was Dr. Raymond A. Moody, Jr., in his book *Life After Life.* Other pioneers in the field included Dr. George G. Ritchie and Dr. Kenneth Ring. Dr. Ring was one of the founders of the Interna-tional Association for Near Death Studies (IANDS).

Love's Eternal Legacy is the result of my work and my judgment. In exercising that judgment I attempted to present the material so as to be consistent with what I learned during my research on NDEs—and to be in concert with my understanding of LDS and Christian scriptures. It is my fervent desire that the material so presented will provide others with the same feelings of love, wonder, and hope which I felt as I listened to people tell of their experiences.

Contents

About the Author

Arvin Gibson has filled numerous teaching and service positions in The Church of Jesus Christ of Latter-day Saints. He has been a bishop, a counselor in a Stake Presidency, a High Counselor, an Elder's Quorum President, and a teacher of numerous classes.

Arvin graduated with a Bachelor of Science Degree in Engineering from the University of California. He took post-graduate courses in engineering and management. For many years he worked and performed research in the field of nuclear engineering. He then joined Utah Power and Light Company where he eventually became an Executive Vice President.

Arvin met his wife, Carol, at the LDS Institute of Religion at the University of California in Berkeley and they were married in 1950. They are the parents of four children and have twelve grandchildren.

Arvin and Carol have both performed extensive research in the field of near-death experiences. They are the authors of three widely-read books on life-after-death experiences which present the results of their numerous interviews: *Glimpses of Eternity, Echoes From Eternity,* and *Journeys Beyond Life.* Arvin and Carol are active in a local chapter of the International Association of Near Death Experiences (IANDS of Utah).

The cover artwork is from an oil painting prepared for this book by florence Susan Comish, of Provo, Utah. The painting, *Love's Eternal Legacy,* depicts the account found on page 153 of this book.

Foreword

Having survived two wives who died of cancer, I have come to know death on very intimate terms. I chose these trials before coming to earth: of that I am sure. But it was my near-death experience in 1963 (recounted in *Glimpses of Eternity)* which prepared me for this 'unfair' turn of events and helped me to continue life, despite the separation and sorrow that ensued. Looking back is instructive, however, and I do not hesitate when I say that it was all in the hands of God and according to His will. (And so is my present wife Signe and the 17 children we are raising from our respective marriages.)

Unfortunately, for those who have not yet experienced the grief that comes from losing a loved one—or who have not had a near-death experience (NDE) themselves—what I testify of has little meaning without the Spirit and without personal revelation. *Love's Eternal Legacy* is a collective testimony of near-death experiences, and the author's intent is to edify and enlarge our perspectives on this very important subject.

In a funeral sermon given October 9, 1843, in honor of Judge James Adams, Joseph Smith described the true perspective all Latter-day Saints should have concerning death:

All men know that they must die. And it is important that we should understand the reasons and causes of our exposure to the vicissitudes of life and of death, and the designs and purposes of God in our coming into the world, our sufferings here, and our departure hence. What is the object of our coming into existence, then dying and falling away, to be here no more? It is reasonable to suppose that God would reveal something in reference to the matter, *and it is a subject we ought to study more than any other* [Italics mine]. We ought to study it day and night, for the world is ignorant in reference to their true condition and relation. If we have any claim on our Heavenly Father for anything, it is for knowledge on this important subject. Could we read and comprehend all that has been written from the days of Adam, on the relation of man to God and angels in a future state, we should know very little about it. Reading the experience of others, or the revelation given to *them*, can never give *us* a comprehensive view of our condition and true relation to God. Knowledge of these things can only be obtained by experience through the ordinances of God set forth for that purpose. *Could you gaze into heaven five minutes, you would know more than you would by reading all that ever was written on the subject.*[1]

Arvin Gibson's *Love's Eternal Legacy* is basically a primer to teach the reader what he or she should already know about death and life hereafter, but which has simply been forgotten. The atmosphere of *Love's Eternal Legacy* is very real to me because of my own NDE. Indeed, when Professor Blair, in the novel, has a vision of his future in which he sees a strange building with towers, and with people inside dressed in white and involved in some type of ceremony, that vision is very similar to what happened to me during my NDE.

Four activities in my life since the death of my wives Lyn and Betsy have helped me to relive the spiritual atmosphere that I had in my NDE. Reading and studying the scriptures is the most obvious. Next, is being aware of all the beauties of nature. The intensity of color and animation on earth are not as great as when I experienced my own NDE, but they come close enough for now.

Another activity that renews the spiritual feeling I got during my NDE is associated with flying and aviation. The human desire to fly, it seems to me, is reminiscent of that time when we were with Father and could travel at will through space just by wishing to be there (as done by the characters in *Love's Eternal Legacy*). The creativity associated with designing and building magnificent

---

1. Smith, Joseph, Jr. *History of the Church of Jesus Christ of Latter-day Saints.* Salt Lake City, Utah: Deseret Book, 1971, 6:50.

flying machines also seems to mirror some of the creativity I felt in the other world during my NDE. For that reason I enjoy building model airplanes.

A final activity that brings, again, the marvelous spiritual feelings I had during my NDE is listening to good music. Several of the characters in *Love's Eternal Legacy* speak of the wondrous ethereal music that they are exposed to, and how great it makes them feel. Music is one of the few things we can take with us and something that we will recognize on the other side, for it is one of those phenomena that follow both natural and eternal laws. In 1990, Marisa Robles, a harpist, discovered that she had cancer. As she dealt with the harsh reality of her cancer she cancelled her musical engagements, spent much time in the garden surrounded by flowers, and repeatedly played Mozart's *Requiem* on the stereo. Here is her reaction:

> That piece gave me a new lease on life. As I lay there thinking, 'What's going to happen to me? How long am I going to live?' I suddenly felt that it really wasn't very important whether I was alive or not, because this music revealed to me the enormous powers of eternity itself. I thought, if the spirit of Mozart is out there somewhere, I wouldn't mind being there too! I didn't feel frightened; it gave me tremendous strength to face something that I couldn't change, and the serenity to accept those first few months of depressing radiotherapy, to accept it all with love, the love that Mozart put into that piece, even though he knew he was dying.[2]

My response to the anticipation of imminent death, I am sure, would be the same as Marisa Robles. I long, again, for the peace

---

2. Robles, Marisa, "Music that Changed Me," *BBC Music Magazine: The Complete Monthly Guide to Classical Music* (April 1994): 106

and love that I felt in my NDE. Yet, that same NDE taught me that each moment of life is extremely precious.

As *Love's Eternal Legacy* eloquently explains, death is but another stage of life, described in the book as the 'fourth birth.' It is a natural part of our eternal lives and going from here to there is no more difficult than going from one room to another. Death, for those who live righteously, can be the most glorious part of life.

It is my hope, reader, that when you finish this book you will feel less fear and more faith in the future. And live love's legacy—with all of your heart, might, mind and strength.

Gary Gillum
Springville, Utah

Preface

When my wife, Carol, and I completed the research and finished the writing of the two books, *Glimpses of Eternity* and *Echoes From Eternity,* I thought that I was through writing about near-death experiences. Work for the two books was a tremendously exhilarating experience, and we would do it again given the same circumstances, but it was also a very exhausting experience, and it was one that I did not feel that I had the energy to continue pursuing.

Many people talked to us after reading one or both of the books about the individuals we had interviewed—those who had undergone a near-death experience. Most of the questions that our readers—and those who really did not read very much—asked us we answered in a chapter of *Echoes From Eternity* which we entitled: "Are the Stories True?" With that chapter, I felt that we had laid the subject to rest.

One of the questions that seemingly would not go away, though, and one that deserves a thorough answer was: "What did you learn from listening to all of those people?" To an extent we answered that question in the second part of the two books. Still, its persistence convinced me that, to many of our readers, I had not adequately responded to the needs of those who read our books.

It was for that reason that I decided to write another book. Thinking, initially, of developing a set of themes such as: I learned that the scriptures are more literal than I had ever supposed; I learned that the Lord's love is a real, a tangible and a personal thing, and it is beyond anything we imagine on earth; I learned that the Light of the Lord really is "the light which is in all things, which giveth life to all things, which is the law by which all things are governed, even the power of God," just as the 88th Section of the Doctrine and Covenants says; I learned that God is more powerful than I had imagined, and He is not circumscribed by laws which science has presumably discovered and which learned men claim to be immutable; I learned that the agency of

11

humans (or free will as it is sometimes called) is so precious that it extends into the premortal existence much more broadly than I had thought; I learned that the veil between this life and the spiritual world is thin, indeed; I learned that . . .

Developing this kind of list helped me to focus on those issues that seemed most important from the stream of knowledge that Carol and I had discovered and drunk from. Unfortunately, our drink was brief, and our thirst seemed unquenchable. In order to expose for others as much of the stream as possible, it became clear that a detailed listing of what we learned would not quench our readers' thirst any more than our brief drinks did for us. We would still be plagued by questions such as: "What do you think life over there is really like?"

In thinking of ways to express the joy, the marvels—and the hell—that our research participants described, I decided that a novel might best respond to those continuing questions. The difficulty with a work of fiction, however, is that it is just that—fiction. If a novel is cast in a historical sense, then some facts may be included in the body of the text, but the reader is never sure what is fact and what is fiction.

Despite these limitations on a work of fiction, it seemed to meet more of the reader needs than any other form of the written word that I could devise. It is for that reason that I offer this work. Be advised, dear reader, that it *is* a work of fiction. It is not intended as a substitute for the scriptures, nor is it intended to supplant more serious research work in the field of near-death experiences.

In creating the story-line for the book, I used, as much as possible, real incidents of persons who have gone through a near-death experience or had some other unusual spiritual experience. In the last chapter, for example, the circumstances behind the recognition by Michael and Laurel that they should marry each other were taken almost directly from another couple who lived through that experience (detailed in the book *In Search of Angels, pp. 146-152)*. On occasion I synthesized an event or series of events from several different near-death experiences. And, as with the previous books, I drew upon my background as a life-time member of The Church of Jesus Christ of Latter-day Saints (Mormon).

One interesting aspect of the book has to do with the words that are used by some of the characters. As noted, where possible the events depicted come from real near-death experiences. During the research period, as I was interviewing the different individuals concerning their experiences, it became apparent that they used particular words repeatedly—and different individuals used the same words. Words such as: *peace, love, joy, light, aura, energy, wholeness, warmth* and *color* were used with such feeling and frequency that they took on a special meaning of their own—a spiritual meaning.

The discussion of *light*, for example, was used so often and with such emotion that I read, again, the 88th Section of the Doctrine and Covenants to better understand what was said there about light. My conclusion was that the scriptural description given in the 88th Section was much more literal than I had ever supposed. Those candidates that I interviewed insisted that the light they saw and felt had beauty beyond belief; it contained emotion, mostly love; when exposed to it, the recipients often had great knowledge; and, above all, the light consisted of energy and power.

Analogous conclusions could be drawn of the other repetitively used words. They seemed to be programmed into the thinking of the individuals I interviewed. As one fourteen-year old girl put it when I asked her why she used the word *peace* so often: "I don't know. It just seems like the right word."

In the text for this book, therefore, I have tried to recreate some of the feeling that I got as I interviewed those choice individuals, by using many of the words that I heard them use with such emotion. Where possible, their emotions are also described.

Because some readers may desire to check into some of the original sources that I used in creating the story line, I have included a rather extensive bibliography. Essentially all of these sources were used as resource material for the book.

Since the book is fiction, though, you are at risk when you read what I have offered. As with many such works, I have interspersed real events with completely imaginary events, and you will have to decide where reality ends and imagination begins. I make no apologies for the work; it represents my best effort to describe an amazing phenomenon—the communication between a spiritual realm and this very physical earthly realm.

As you read what I have written you will also have to decide whether any of what I have to offer is of value. It may be that you will decide the work is the musing of a rather addled and aging author. On the other hand, it may be that you will ascribe it to the enlightened inspiration of an individual who briefly glimpsed eternity through the eyes of those who have been there. It probably is something between these two extremes.

In any event, in deciding which of the many possibilities this work is, please know that my earnest desire is to paint a picture that is helpful, not hurtful. In this world racked with fear, uncertainty, death, destruction, cynicism, and despair, there seems to be an urgent need for messages of hope. This fictional work is offered in that context. And may you learn to love Laura, Mathias, Janis, Alma, Professor Blair, Barnabas, . . . as I did in writing about them. Happy reading!

Arvin S. Gibson

Major Characters

Laura, a female spirit awaiting her turn on Earth.

Mathias, a male spirit debating whether to go to Earth or to some other less fearsome planet.

Gallexus, a male spirit who has completed his Earthly mission, and now is a teacher of other spirits.

Brother Pratt, a superior male spirit, having completed his Earthly mission where he was known as Parley P. Pratt. He is now involved in preparing others for high callings.

Sister Thankful, a superior female spirit, having completed her Earthly mission where she was known as Thankful Pratt, the first wife of Parley P. Pratt. She is now involved in preparing others for high callings.

Brother Olvin, a patriarch in the Blair family line. One of the few Blairs who became members of The Church of Jesus Christ of Latter-day Saints. Having completed his Earthly mission, and become a superior spirit, he is now busy helping others in his line to advance.

Martha Blair (sometimes known as Mother Blair), the Earthly wife of Olvin Blair. Since the death of her husband, she has become actively involved in helping her children and her grandchildren.

Brother Brigham, a superior male spirit with substantial priesthood power. Having completed his Earthly mission as Brigham Young, the prophet, he is now involved in decisions bearing on the future development of spirits.

Alma Pratt, a young engineer serving on Earth as a husband, a father, the manager of the Hunter Power Station in Utah, and the LDS Bishop of the Price 10th Ward. He is a descendant of Parley P. Pratt.

Janis Pratt (previously Janis Miller), a young woman serving on Earth as a wife, a mother, and Stake Family History Specialist. She is a descendant of Brigham Young. Anxious to have another child, she is uncertain about becoming pregnant because of a serious health problem with diabetes.

Norma Miller, the Earthly mother of Janis Pratt, currently living in Phoenix, Arizona.   She is very involved with her grandchildren.

Jeremy and **Sherman Pratt**, the nine- and four-year-old sons of Alma and Janis Pratt.

Jim Blair, a young man serving on Earth as a husband, a father, the maintenance manager of the Hunter Power Station in Utah, and the Executive Secretary of the Price 10th Ward. He is one of the sons of Olvin and Martha Blair.

Lori Blair, a young woman serving on Earth as the wife of Jim Blair, a mother, and Spiritual Living Teacher in the Relief Society of the Price 10th Ward. She is pregnant with her fourth child and actively involved in searching out her husband's genealogy.

Jeff, **Alice** and **Ruth Blair**, the twelve-, nine- and seven-year-old children of Jim and Lori Blair.

Alvin Blair, a young man serving on Earth as a husband, a father, and administrative assistant in the General Electric nuclear engineering facility located in San Jose, California. He is an active member of the LDS Church and the youngest son of Olvin and Martha Blair.

Sue Blair, a young woman serving on Earth as a wife, a mother, and an active member of the LDS Church. She would like to have a boy to complement her two girls.

Leah and **Rose Blair**, the five- and three-year-old daughters of Alvin and Sue Blair.

John Blair, serving on Earth as a husband and as a Professor of Philosophy at the University of California in Berkeley. The oldest son of Olvin and Martha Blair, he is proud of his accomplishments. He is a dedicated aetheist.

Barbara Blair, serving on Earth as a wife and as a Professor of Law at the University of California in Berkeley. She would like to have a child, but she is reluctant to press the issue with her husband, Professor John Blair, who suggests that she concentrate on her professional career.

Barnabas, a spirit awaiting birth on Earth. He has accepted a future calling as a prophet of Father and the Son.

Chapter 1

KOLOB-1; A BEAUTIFUL PLACE

If you could hie to Kolob in the twinkling of an eye,
And then continue onward with that same speed to fly,
Do you think that you could ever, through all eternity,
Find out the generation where Gods began to be? [1]

The two natural satellites orbiting Kolob-1 were high in the sky, and Laura responded to the beauty with a quiet prayer of thanksgiving. Kolob-Star had sunk below the horizon, and other distant stars were visible in the slightly pink sky that reflected the energy field which encompassed the planet.

Rising from her kneeling prayer position, Laura reflected again on how grateful she was for having been assigned to the planet Kolob-1. The other planets that orbited Kolob-Star, such as Kolob-2 and Justin-3, were beautiful also, and they, too, gave opportunities for growth, but not like Kolob-1. More importantly, she would not be as close to Mathias as she was. Mathias was somewhat less advanced in his progression than Laura, and he often made different choices than she, but the glow of his spirit was real, and she loved him dearly.

Pondering some of the things she had learned since arriving on Kolob-1, Laura made the most of her Quiet. Some of the others

---

1 Phelps, William W., 1792-1872, *Hymns of The Church of Jesus Christ of Latter-day Saints*, Published by The Church of Jesus Christ of Latter-day Saints, Salt Lake City, Utah, 1985, p. 284.

18

had to receive instruction on how to use the Quiet, but not Laura. She let her thoughts drift through the many things that she had learned, and she intermixed her meditation with study of the History, and with prayer.

As a location for her Quiet, Laura chose different outdoor locations. Mathias, Skosh, Debrush and some of the others preferred the Library, or other indoor places, but Laura loved the feeling of space and openness that she got from the outdoors, not to mention the ease of absorbing energy from the planetary energy field.

On this particular revolution of Kolob-1, Laura had willed herself atop Mount Isaiah. From Isaiah she could see the distant Sea of Life, which reflected the pale pink of the sky. Intervening between Mount Isaiah and the Sea of Life was the enormous Valley of the Son with its beautiful rivers, waterfalls, gardens and pathways. Life abounded in the valley, and Laura could feel the energy and joy that radiated from the various forms of life there. The colors were spectacular, and each tree, flower and shrub seemed to be singing of the joy of life.

A large group of people was gathered near Lake Jacob, and music was emanating from them. It was a wondrous ethereal sound that filled Laura with a sense of eager anticipation. Knowing that this group of spirits were soon to choose their birth into a more physical world, where their ability to respond to that environment would be tested, Laura was thrilled. She hoped that she would be as ready and anxious as they now were when it was her turn.

Occasionally, during her Quiet, Laura was able to catch a glimpse of exactly what the new world would be like. This moment was one of those occasions; Laura saw herself on a world, less colorful than Kolob-1, but still with a degree of beauty. Watching the vision unfold before her, she could almost feel the excitement as she witnessed herself talking, with some amount of emotion, to a man and woman. It seemed that she was upset because they were late for some function she was to take part in—a school function. Studying the vision carefully, Laura began to understand what was happening when the vision faded.

These glimpses of the future were almost as frustrating as they were helpful. Her teacher had explained that, as she became more advanced and used her Quiet correctly, she would see and understand more of what could happen to her in the new world. She knew that these visions of the future, although very real in their appearance and feel, were only a probable outcome based on a series of events. If she, or others, did not behave in a predictable manner, then the outcomes could be different. Presenting themselves in visions, these different outcomes were sometimes puzzling, particularly those where she saw herself hurting someone else.

There was so much about the birth-world that Laura still did not understand—particularly Earth with its many risks. She knew of The Plan developed by Elohim and Jehovah, and she knew that Lucifer disagreed with The Plan and was cast out from their presence, but still . . .

Laura's thoughts became almost a prayer. *How could I possibly hurt someone else. Even though my memory of my life here was lost, I know that I could not hurt anyone—why would I want to? Why would I get upset in speaking to someone else, just because I was late for something? Late? I still don't understand how time works. And the idea of measuring it seems absurd. I know that Teacher Gallexus taught us how valuable our time in the new world would be, but . . . ?*

Reflecting again on what she knew to be true, Laura referred to the History and called up a vision of the War. She saw, again, the myriads of those who agreed with The Plan, as presented by Jehovah, the Son. Lucifer, the Son of the Morning, and approximately a third of all those present, disagreed. Objecting to the part of The Plan that allowed risk—and freedom of choice—in the birth-world, this third of Elohim's children wanted Lucifer's alternative plan. The Lucifer plan provided for no risk, and salvation for all, but without freedom of choice and with all glory to Lucifer. Jehovah pointed out that the Lucifer plan would not provide for the growth of individuals that Elohim's plan would, but Lucifer's followers would not listen.

Watching the History vision unfold, Laura felt again of the agony as Elohim the Father and Jehovah the Son cast out Lucifer—who became Satan—and his followers from the spirit system. They were first cast into outer darkness. After Earth and other planets and stars were formed, Satan and his followers were then allowed to visit Earth and to have influence there. When Kolob and its planetary system were formed, though, they were not allowed to visit there, where Elohim and Jehovah dwelt. The misery of the rejected beings was felt by all—they would never have the opportunity of receiving physical bodies and experiencing a birth-life as would those who joined with Jehovah.

Feeling the exhilaration and exultant joy of the trillions of beings who accepted The Plan, Laura loved this portion of the History. She saw herself, and all of her other brothers and sisters, as they shouted for joy, and she felt again the wonderful Spirit that confirmed the rightness of her choice.

Sometimes, during her Quiet, Laura joined some of the others in the Library. The Word was there, in books of the history of different worlds. Earth's history was particularly interesting to Laura. She often studied The Word, as it was recorded by prophets who lived on the Earth, and she wondered why many now living on Earth did not believe what was written in the books. Her teachers tried to explain it, but she was still puzzled.

Kolob-Star was rising on the 270 degree horizon when Laura completed her Quiet. The sky was a beautiful blue-white with touches of pink. Thousands of birds were flying toward the rising star, as they replenished their energy from the star's rays. Flying into the rays, the bird's joyful cries were as a melodic symphony playing softly in the atmosphere. Laura joined the birds and sang with exuberance.

Ending her Quiet with prayer, Laura thought of Mathias and wondered what he was about. Instantly, she was beside him walking in the gardens and lawns of the Library. Thousands of people were entering and leaving the gigantic buildings in an attitude of reverent hush. Usually the radiant sheen of the buildings, and the glowing green of the lawns attracted Laura's attention, but not on this occasion. Even Mathias's welcoming smile did not reassure her.

It was Mathias's aura that disturbed her—the glowing intensity was distinctly less than the last meeting with him. Mathias felt of her concern, and he responded with mind-talk. *I know, it's not as bright as before. It's just that I'm not sure that I'm ready yet. I do love you, Laura, and I know that we talked of going to Earth together, but . . .*

Laura interrupted by vocally saying: "Speak orally, Mathias. You know that Teacher Gallexus instructed us to practice speaking with our mouths. That's the only way we'll be able to communicate on earth—except for prayer."

"I know," Mathias said orally, with some difficulty, "but it seems so cumbersome. That's one of the things that bothers me about Earth. Everything has to be so hard. Things are much easier on Krasak-3 in the Epsus Galaxy, and the Son's love extends to that sphere as well as it does to Earth. Why can't we go there?"

Laura felt hurt, and Mathias could feel her hurt. Trying to reassure her of his love through her mind, he began: *You know that I love you, and I want to be with you . . .*

"Stop it, Mathias. It's not always best to take the easy way. After all, Lucifer's plan would have been the easiest one of all. All the hard things would have been eliminated. Why didn't we choose it?"

"I know, but I'm not talking about Lucifer's plan. My concern is with Earth. You remember what it was like when Teacher Gallexus showed us a vision of it. Didn't you feel of the horror of the place?"

"Yes. And I have some of the same feelings of dread that you do. But in that same vision I also felt of the enormous sense of growth and development that came from Earth. There's nothing comparable in any of the other places we could go. Look at the superior beings that come from there. How many Marys, or Abrahams, or Moronis, or Joseph Smiths come from Krasak-3?"

"Well, why do we all have to be such superior beings? Teacher Gallexus also told us that other, less advanced souls, would achieve a degree of happiness in their heaven that was all they desired. What's wrong with that?"

"You don't really mean that, Mathias. I've watched you help other spirits grow and develop. And you were the one that wanted us to be assigned to Kolob-1, where, as you said, we would learn the most. Well, the same is true of Earth. It's just another step, and the most important step of all, in our progression. Would you be satisfied with anything less than that?"

"Maybe not, but perhaps . . . maybe I should attend another class for awhile. You seem so anxious to move ahead, and possibly I should try something else until I feel the strength that you seem to have."

Mathias could feel Laura's anguish for him, and he loved her for it. She began to communicate in mind-talk. *I'm sorry Mathias, I didn't mean to push you into a position where you felt uncomfortable. It's just, as you say, that I'm anxious to get on with the next stage in our development—birth-life. Of course you can take a different class than I do until you feel more secure. In fact, I can ask for a new assignment while you attend a different class. Teacher Gallexus asked me if I'd help him in a new project that he has been assigned. I'm not sure what it is, but he promised me it would be interesting.*

Mathias moved close to Laura, and their two spirit forms embraced. Their energy fields merged and they felt of each other's love together with a sense of peace. It was not the enormous love and peace that they felt when The Son was near—or when they were around Father and Mother. But they knew that the peace and joy they experienced in each other's arms was derived from the love that came from their elder brother. Laura also knew that this was but a fraction of the love they would enjoy if they were true to their estate on Earth.

Laura willed herself back on Mount Isaiah when Mathias left. Contemplating their meeting, she wondered at her own anxiety. It was wrong, she knew, for her to impose her will on Mathias.

Freedom of choice was a key part of the Father's Plan, and yet she couldn't resist attempting to restrict the choices of Mathias. It was because she loved him so and wanted the best for him in every-thing, and yet . . . ? How could it be the best if she imposed her will on the one she loved?

The love she had for Mathias was real. It stemmed from their initial work together during the Great War. But during that time, Mathias was such a stalwart warrior in defense of the Father and the Son. She was sure, then, that Mathias would always be a firm defender of The Plan. What had caused his change? Was it she and her pushy determination to proceed to Earth that had caused his change? The thought that she had retarded the progress of Mathias through her actions was a fearful one—even more fearful than the thought of Earth and its inherent risks. What could she do to make amends?

Looking at the beauty of her surroundings, Laura began a prayer: *Please, Father, help Mathias to understand the full beauty of thy Plan. And help me to be patient. Bless us both that we may have the courage to select those options that will lead to our greatest growth. And if it be thy will, bless us that we might both select Earth for our birth-life.*

I thank thee for Jehovah, thy Son, who became Jesus Christ the Savior of the Earth. I thank thee also for the challenges that we will have to meet during our birth-life, and help us to resist the evil influences of Satan. Please give me wisdom that I might not force Mathias to do something that will hurt him.

I thank thee for all of my blessings. . . . In the name of thy Son, Amen.

Completing her prayer, Laura let her spirit soar over the Valley of the Son. From her vantage point above the walls of the canyon she could see the mighty Falls of Adam as they cascaded in a splashing foam into the river below. Unimaginable colors met her view, and she could see and feel of the abounding life in the canyon. The atmosphere through which she floated smelled of the living canyon. It seemed that the very rocks and the river were singing for joy. Could anything on Earth, or anywhere else, match the beauty, the love, the joy, the peace that she now beheld?

Chapter 2

CLASS TIME

For by him were all things created, that are in heaven, and that are in earth, visible and invisible, whether they be thrones, or dominions, or principalities, or powers: all things were created by him, and for him: And he is before all things, and by him all things consist. [1]

The class was already in session when Laura arrived. Smiling at her as she entered, Teacher Gallexus mind-transmitted a quick synopsis of what had been covered in her absence. Then he continued orally instructing the class in Earth characteristics.

"So, you see, Earth was formed by Elohim, the Father, Jehovah, the Son, and Michael (who became Adam) in such a way as to emphasize physical characteristics, and to deemphasize spiritual characteristics. When you go to Earth, your memory of a spiritual life before Earth life will be obliterated. You will have The Word from prophets and from The History, and there will be prayer, but many people will not believe The Word."

"How can they not believe?" asked Sherney.

"Because, aside from the written Word, there will be no evidence that you existed before Earth life or that you will exist after it."

"Won't the Earth itself, and all the living creatures in it be evidence of the living Father and his Son?" Laura asked.

---

1 *The Bible*. Colossians 1:16-17.

"That's a good question. The problem is, in order to protect agency, or free will, knowledge of life after life on Earth must be very obscure. Thus, when you reach the end of your life, as with all other living forms of life, your bodies will die. People will see what happens after death, and many will think that's all there is."

"Please explain death, again, Teacher Gallexus. It sounds so ghastly, I'm not sure that I understand it," Shamz requested.

Gallexus smiled. "To those on earth who do not believe in The Word, it *will* be ghastly. At your appointed time your body will experience pain and illness, or because of an accident it will not function properly, and it will cease to live. At death, the spirit will leave the body and return to Father. Other living people who witness this death will not be able to see the spirit, except in exceptional circumstances. To them, the body will become cold and the limbs will fail to move. With time, the body will decay to dust. Viewing the decayed body of a dead person, with its accompanying heavy odor of decay, many will be convinced that this is the end destiny of all living beings—to be destroyed with no consciousness of ever having existed."

"How does pain work?" asked Shamz.

"It's understandable that you cannot know what pain is; you've never experienced it. When I went to Earth, and other Teachers had explained the idea to me, I only dimly understood what they were talking about. Yet, when it happened to me it was a vivid experience, and it was not pleasant.

"You say that pain is unpleasant. How can anything that's unpleasant be good?" asked Shamz.

"It's good in the sense that it alerts you to problems that need to be corrected to protect your body. It also is a great teaching tool to see how well you respond to this form of adversity. Satan and his followers will be there trying to get you to surrender to the pain. But that's the subject of a different lesson."

Gallexus searched the room using thought transference to find out how the students were receiving his instruction. Most of them seemed to be absorbing it reasonably well. He knew from his thought query of Laura that Mathias was absent and would have trouble accepting some of the ideas. He wondered if Mathias would be ready for Earth when Laura left. She was so anxious for them to go together. Considering these issues, he looked again at Laura, and she signalled a question.

"Yes, Laura?"

"I still wonder why people on Earth disbelieve in Father and the Son."

"Earthlings, at least those who don't accept The Word, only know what they can observe. Many of the Earth scientists are good at making observations. And a significant proportion of them reject the idea of God."

Gallexus could tell that Laura was frustrated. He wanted the class to know of her frustration, so he asked: "What troubles you, Laura?"

"I object to your characterization of God as an idea. The Father and the Son are not an idea—they are real, and they created us and everything in the universe."

Smiling to himself at Laura's vigorous defense of God, Gallexus said: "You're right, Laura, but you're thinking in terms of a spiritual being. Put yourself in the position of the Earth bound scientist who knows what his science teaches him and is skeptical of anything else."

"But the *mind* of God is made known to humans through The Word. All they have to do is read the History. Furthermore, there are prophets to tell them the mind of God. Surely that should help them understand what God is saying."

"That would be true if they read and believed the History, or if they listened to the prophets. A large fraction of them, though, do not believe the History or the prophets."

"How do they think that the Earth and all living things in it came to be?"

"They're not sure. Many scientists say that it may have happened by chance, and that life developed over several billion Earth-years in a spontaneous evolutionary manner. They argue that single-celled life forms could have started in some Earthly primordial mixture of chemicals, and that given enough time these life forms eventually evolved into the more complex types of life found on earth. Ultimately, they say, some of these life forms became human with all of the characteristics that we know . . ."

Gallexus was interrupted by the laughing of the class members, and some of them, Gallexus knew by his mind reading, were puzzled. Laura asked: "Do you mean that they believe this happened completely by chance, without the help of the Father or the Son?"

"That's what they say."

The whole class laughed. Roshfez asked: "Why is it so difficult for them to accept The Word, and to know that the Father and the Son formed man in their own image, as The Word says?"

"Because then they'd have to accept the entire Word, including the fact that the Father and the Son, whom they cannot see, really exist. They'd have to believe in the words of the prophets, and many would have to change the way they're living to match what the prophets tell them. They don't want to do that. Besides, Satan and his followers are continually influencing people to disbelieve The Word and the prophets. Because of these influences, many people lose most or all of the spirit of the Son, and they ignore or are cut off from the prompting of the Holy Ghost."

"How sad," said Roshfez.

"In a way, yes. It's sad that the knowledge and progression of some individuals are thereby retarded. The good thing, though, is that the agency of all individuals is protected by allowing each individual to choose his or her own way. As you know, a major part of The Plan is the principle of agency, or free will. In order for people to progress, under The Plan, they must accept some of what the prophets tell them with faith—without perfect knowledge.

"There's much instruction given in The Word on faith. You recall the incident from the History when Thomas, one of the Savior's disciples, would not believe that Jesus had been resurrected, even though others had told him about it, until he saw the Lord himself. What Thomas said is recorded in the History in this manner: 'Except I shall see in his hands the print of the nails, and put my finger into the print of the nails, and thrust my hand into his side, I will not believe. . . .' When the Son appeared to Thomas, do you remember what he said to Thomas?"

Laura volunteered: "He said, 'Thomas, because thou hast seen me, thou hast believed: blessed are they that have not seen, and yet have believed.' Your point, Teacher Gallexus, must be that the scientists now on Earth must be similar to Thomas. Is that right?"

"That's exactly right. Except that Thomas had one important advantage that the scientists don't have. He lived with the Savior during the Savior's Earthly life; he saw the miracles, and he felt of the spirit. Still, he didn't believe when the Son died that the Son had risen from the dead—until he was able to get complete proof. If that was true of Thomas, one of the Twelve, then is it any wonder that many Earthlings don't believe?

"Before we close this lesson, let me call your attention, again, to faith. It's an extremely important part of The Plan, and because of its importance there are many references to faith in The Word.

"This should be enough of the lesson for the moment. Now, most of you have other assignments and you should attend to them. Laura, will you remain after class for a while?"

After the class dispersed, Teacher Gallexus came and sat next to Laura. She loved to be near him and feel of his spirit. Having completed his Earthly life mission, although he was not yet resurrected, Gallexus was an advanced spirit with priesthood power. He was one of the superior ones, and his aura was a bright one reflecting his power and glory.

Communicating his love as he joined Laura, Gallexus vocally said: "I spoke with you briefly about a possible new assignment."

"Yes you did, Gallexus, and I'm looking forward to whatever you'd like me to do."

"It's not from me. Brother Brigham wishes to talk to you. Could you meet with him at the Library when Kolob-Star breaks the horizon next?"

"Brother Brigham? He's so busy, ordinarily, working with those who've completed their Earth-life missions. I wonder what he wants with me?"

"He'll explain it when you meet. May the Spirit be with you."

"Thank you Gallexus—and may the Spirit be with you."

Laura was overwhelmed by the thought of meeting with Brother Brigham. Knowing of his position and responsibilities she wondered what on Kolob-1 he could want with her. Perhaps it would be a chastisement for the way she attempted to manage Mathias. Surely, though, Brother Brigham would understand that her motivation was pure—it was because of her love for Mathias, . . . or was it?

Laura's thoughts became, almost, a prayer. *Why do I get so confused when it comes to Mathias? He is such a marvelous spirit, and I love him for his tenderness, for his loving loyalty, and for the independence of his ideas. Yet, when he expresses those ideas, I try to impose my will upon him. The Plan is wonderful in granting agency to all of us, but where it counts the most—with the one I love—I cannot yield my will to his needs. Brother Brigham would be right if he chastised me. Teacher Gallexus is correct, we should learn from our mistakes. How will I learn the lessons on Earth if I can't learn them here, where everything is much clearer? Maybe I should . . . yes, I should get together with Mathias and let him know how much I love him—and apologize for the way I have treated him.*

Having reached this firm conclusion, as was typical of Laura, she was ready for action. She immediately transmitted a thought to Mathias: *Mathias, love, please join me on Mount Isaiah. I need to speak with you.*

Mathias had just completed another class on Krasak-3 when he received Laura's transmission. He was much enthused by what he had learned in class, and he wanted to tell Laura about it. On the other hand, he was not sure he was ready to face up to Laura's arguments of why they should go to Earth. He needed to have at least one more class concerning Krasak-3 to better persuade her that there were attractive alternatives to Earth. Laura could be so positive in her beliefs, sometimes, that she was difficult to communicate with—especially if they had to use the awkward Earth way of speaking, by voice.

It wasn't always thus. Mathias thought back to the time when they had all shouted for joy over the acceptance of the Father's plan, or The Plan as it came to be known. Laura and he had been assigned to work with those who, although they accepted The Plan, still harbored some reluctance to embrace all aspects of it. It was for those individuals that other planets had been created, such as Krasak-3, which were not as risky as was Earth with its more complete freedom of choice.

During that wonderful embryonic period, Laura gladly followed Mathias's lead as he showed her ways to help others choose directions that would be most beneficial for their growth. Her boundless energy and determination to succeed became an ensign for others to follow. And Mathias loved her for it.

It was only later, when Laura's enthusiasm for the work became an . . . yes, her enthusiasm became an obsession. Anything or anyone that stood in the way of what she perceived to be right she felt obligated to change—until that thing or individual conformed to her way of thinking. At least, that was the way Mathias saw it. Perhaps he was unfairly judging Laura, and he knew that judgment by him in any form was wrong.

Partly as a reaction to Laura's insistence on proceeding with the Earth option Mathias began to consider other options. He observed, for example, that good spirits who spent their birth-life on Krasak-3 returned with boundless joy and happiness, much as those from Earth did. They still had a large measure of the Son's love, and they were able to continue, within certain limits, with their future growth.

Laura was right, however, there weren't many you could point to from Krasak-3 who had the outstanding characteristics of many of the individuals returning from Earth. On the other hand—and Mathias wished he had reminded Laura about this fact—there were far fewer individuals returning from Krasak-3 who had failed in their righteous goals. Actually, some of the spirits from Krasak-3 referred jokingly to Earth as the "failure factory."

Initially, as he and Laura worked together to show others what their options were, both Laura and Mathias had explained that the greater risks of Earth were more than offset by the greater opportunities for growth. Later, as Mathias listened to those few from Krasak-3 who had accomplished a great deal in their birth-life missions, he wasn't so sure. The fraction of those from Krasak-3 consigned to various forms of hell was far less than the fraction of those who had been to Earth. Not that Mathias expected to go to hell—although he did wish that he knew more about hell.

Part of the problem was that spirits, prior to their birth-lives, were expected to make major choices concerning their future estates on Krasak-3, Earth, and other planets. And they had to make those choices without complete understanding of the risks involved. The idea of pain, for example, and a physical body that could feel pain, or be damaged by illness—Mathias had never felt pain. How could anyone make an intelligent choice of possible future events when there was no way to anticipate what the reaction to those events would be?

Laura embraced these concepts with eager anticipation, and with complete confidence in her ability to deal with all risks. Her faith, Mathias knew, was great, and he loved her for it. The beauty of her beliefs was in their simplicity. When he was around her, he too felt of the strength and beauty of her position. It was only when he considered the risks involved that his faith wavered.

Fear was a concept from Earth that many of his instructors had told Mathias about. As they explained it, excessive fear could retard an individual's growth, even leading to aberrant behavior. Fear in moderation, on the other hand, could sharpen the senses and help protect an individual from spiritual or physical danger.

Although Mathias understood that without a physical body the emotional trauma associated with extreme fear would not be possible, he wondered if his doubts and anxiety concerning the risks of future physical life were not a form of fear. At times he found himself completely frustrated by the thought of making choices that would have an impact on his entire future. During those periods he found it best to enter into a Quiet—and contemplate pleasant subjects, such as his love for Laura.

This was one of those times, so Mathias decided against responding to Laura's request for him to join her, at least for a while. He needed more information concerning the various choices that he must ultimately make. He would meet with Laura when he felt more secure about the effect that their different choices would have on them. In the interim period he would concentrate on what he could learn from his various classes.

Entering into his Quiet, Mathias thought of Laura and transmitted a message of love. He knew that she would receive it with joy, and he hoped that she would accept the message with understanding and forgiveness.

Chapter 3

A NEW CALLING

'Tis hers, with heav'nly influence
To wield a mighty power divine—
To shield the path of innocence
And virtue's sacred worth define.
'Tis hers to cultivate the germs
Of all the faculties for good,
That constitute the Godlike forms
Of perfect man and womanhood.[1]

Ending her Quiet with prayer, Laura watched as the first rays of Kolob-Star broke the horizon. It was always a thrilling sight when the star appeared in the sky, and Laura never tired of it. This rotation of Kolob-1 was notably exciting because she was to meet with Brother Brigham.

Having met Brother Brigham previously, Laura knew of his extraordinary achievements. He was one of the superior spirits who had completed a triumphant mission on Earth. Brother Brigham had succeeded Brother Joseph, when Brother Joseph was martyred, as the Son's prophet on Earth. Knowing that these two remarkable spirits had assignments to organize the teaching of many spirits who had completed their Earthly mission, she wondered what Brother Brigham wanted with her.

---

1 Snow, Eliza, 1804-1887, *What Is, and What Is Not for Woman*, "Out of the Best Books, Volume 4," Deseret Book Company, Salt Lake City, Utah 1968, p. 267.

As Kolob-Star began its rise in the sky, Laura willed herself to the Library. The beautiful buildings that composed the Library shone in their early morning splendor. Surrounding the buildings were flowers, shrubs, lawns, and trees, and the colors were beyond description. Every blade of grass appeared flawlessly in its correct place, and the grass, shrubs and flowers seemed to speak to Laura with animation. She responded with her love for all the life she saw and felt.

Entering one of the beautifully columned buildings with an intricately carved oak door, she moved to a circular staircase made of a varicolored stone material that gave off its own light. Many people were quietly passing in a large hallway next to the rising staircase. In addition to the light from the glowing stone materials, a large skylight in an elevated domed ceiling illuminated much of the interior. Frescoes of varied colors illustrated historical events from Earth on different walls, and a soft symphony of sound seemed to fill the atmosphere.

Starting up the staircase, Laura noticed a man with his arm full of books descending toward her. She recognized him as Brother Benjamin, one of the Teachers who had instructed a class that Laura had attended. On Earth, Brother Benjamin had been known as Benjamin Franklin, and he had accomplished much before the end of his mission there. As they passed, Brother Benjamin smiled and extended his love.

Entering a room at the top of the staircase, Laura saw several men and women seated around a large elaborately carved table. They were all dressed in white robes, as was Laura, but their robes glowed more than hers. Their auras were especially bright, so she knew that these were some of the superior ones. Seated at the head of the table was Brother Brigham. All the men rose when Laura entered, and Brother Brigham smiled a welcome. He invited her to be seated next to him.

Seated on the other side of Brother Brigham was a tall, dark-haired spirit with an aura that almost matched that of Brother Brigham. He smiled his love to Laura. She had a vague sense of having known him before.

Brother Brigham began mind-talking to Laura and to the group. *Laura, I think you know most of those here. All except for Barnabas, who's sitting next to me, have completed their Earthly missions. The individual at the opposite end of the table is Brother Parley. The rest of the people, except for Barnabas, are Earthly descendants of Brother Parley.*

Several of us have been watching your progress with your different teachers. Teacher Gallexus is especially pleased with your knowledge and understanding of The Plan. Because of that progress, the Son has asked that I interview you for a special calling.

Laura was overwhelmed with emotion. Instead of a chastisement from Brother Brigham for her deportment with Mathias, which she half expected, she had been singled out by the Son for a special calling. She knew that the Son watched each of Father's children with care—still, she was amazed that she should have been selected for a special calling.

Brother Brigham continued: *The calling, if you accept it, will be to become the mother of a prophet on Earth. There's much risk associated with the calling, and the consequences of failure could be devastating to you and many others, but the blessings from success are limitless. How would you feel about such a call? Would you consider it? . . .*

How would she feel? Would she consider it? In a manner so characteristic of Laura, she enthusiastically and immediately embraced the idea. She could scarcely contain herself. She mind-transmitted: *I'd be thrilled beyond words, beyond thought, to accept the calling, but am I ready? More importantly, am I worthy? And what about Mathias? I was hoping that he and I could go to Earth together, or almost together, and perhaps . . . perhaps we could find ourselves and become husband and wife.*

Smiling at her reaction, Brother Brigham thought transmitted: *First, yes you are worthy, and second, no, you are not yet ready. There would be much distinctive training before you could leave.*

Concerning Mathias, we are aware of how you feel about each other, and it's possible that it could work out, but much depends on Mathias. As you know, he recently stopped attending Earth classes so that he could attend classes for Krasak-3. His progress, frankly, is not as great as your progress is. If he can't keep up with you, it would be better if someone else received the calling to be father of the prophet.

Speaking orally, Brother Parley interjected: "Laura could be born into our family line whether or not Mathias became the father. We could watch him and see how he progresses—assuming that he accepts such a call—and we could prompt him on Earth with help from angels."

"That's true, Parley," Brother Brigham said, "and it might be useful to see how he reacts to Laura's calling before we extend a call to him. What do you think, Laura?"

"Oh yes, Brother Brigham, give me a chance to talk to Mathias. What did you mean, though, when you said there would be distinctive training for me?"

"In order to increase the likelihood of your success we need to expose you to different situations before you go to Earth so that you can learn as much as possible about life on Earth. It's true that when you leave here you will forget most of what you learned, but if you're spiritually in tune there'll be flashes of recognition when you experience certain spiritual events on Earth. And, of course, there will be prayer so that you can call upon Father."

"What sort of situations will I be exposed to that'll help me learn of birth-life?"

"You've almost finished your class time, so there'll only be a few more sessions there. We'll send you to Earth, though, so that you can see the family that has been called to serve as your parents—and so that you can see how Satan attempts to thwart The Plan. You'll also have an opportunity to work with some of the spirits who've completed their Earthly missions. Finally, you'll be allowed to choose many of the circumstances under which you'll serve your Earthly mission."

Pondering what she had just been told, Laura again accepted the assignment with exuberance. She understood many of the risks involved, but in her characteristic way, she had complete confidence in her ability to respond to those risks in an appropriate manner. More importantly, she knew that she could call upon

Father for help when she needed it. She was excited about the prospect of making choices that would have an impact on her future life. A puzzling aspect, though, was why she would be allowed to go to Earth before her birth-life.

Laura commented: "I thought that those spirits who had not yet completed their Earthly missions were confined to this sphere—they couldn't travel to other planets and mingle with those who were still working out their progression. It was my understanding that only superior beings—who had successfully completed their Earthly missions—could visit other planets. In fact, I thought that only such advanced spirits, after completing their Earthly sojourns, could teach those who still needed to be taught."

"Generally, this is true. You should know, though, Laura, that you *are* an advanced spirit. Your aura, and the spirit of peace and love that you exude testify to that. But, yes, in circumstances such as this, the Son allows neophyte spirits to do what more advanced beings would normally do. You have a unique calling, and we want to help you in every way we can. As you know, Michael helped to create the Earth before he was assigned there as Adam for his Earthly mission. And, of course, Jehovah, the Son, visited Adam, Moses, the Brother of Jared, and many other prophets before he commenced his Earthly mission."

Laura was silent as she contemplated what she had been told. She felt an immense outpouring of love from all of those present. Then she felt a singular communication from Barnabas, the spirit who had been sitting quietly next to Brigham. His name, she knew, meant Son of Prophecy, and she wondered whether that had anything to do with a future mission he might undertake. As he began his mind-talk, she recognized him.

Yes, Laura, I was with you when we helped Jehovah against Lucifer. We worked together to help cast out those who followed Lucifer. Now it appears that we will work together again. I have been assigned, if I am true to my calling, to be your Earthly son, and to be a prophet for the Savior of the Earth.

Exchanging love with Barnabas, and others around the table, Laura felt of the ebullience of those present. They all shared a sense of exhilaration and eager anticipation. Brother Brigham called on Sister Thankful, Parley's eternal wife, to offer a prayer, and the meeting was adjourned.

Mathias had just completed another class session on Krasak-3 when Laura met him. Enthusiastic about what he had learned in his classes, he thought transmitted: *Things are much easier on Krasak-3, Laura. There's direct communication with spirits from Father, and Satan only has limited power. The devastating wars of Earth, and other similar tragedies, simply do not happen there. Even the climate is more moderate.*

I know that, Mathias, but agency is not the same as on Earth either. It's true that there are fewer cataclysmic events on Krasak-3, but there are also fewer opportunities for individual growth.

Mathias paused as he considered how to respond. Knowing that Laura was fully committed to life on Earth, he so wanted her to understand his point of view. Why was it that when he was around the person he loved so much it was almost impossible to communicate in a manner that she understood? If they had difficulty understanding each other on Kolob-1, what would happen on Earth as they tried to speak—presuming that they found each other?

After some careful thought, Mathias transmitted the message: *The Son's love extends to Krasak-3, Laura, as it does for Earth, and there's opportunity for advancement, just not as much nor as rapid as on Earth. But what's wrong with that? People are still happy who complete their birth-missions on Krasak-3. What's so important about the agency of Earth?*

Laura tried hard not to let her emotions be transmitted to Mathias. Still, he couldn't help but know that she would be disappointed. Why was it necessary to explore the same old issues so many times? Surely, Mathias understood the benefits of Earth. She transmitted: *Of course people are happy who complete their birth-missions on Krasak-3. Even those who finish their missions on Earth and are assigned to the Terrestrial or Telestial Kingdoms, will have a degree of happiness. But it won't be the same as those who measure up for the Celestial Kingdom. You mentioned that Satan is less free on Krasak-3 to interfere with The Plan. Do you remember how one of our teachers, Lehi, explained the nature of opposition on Earth, Satan's role in providing opposition, and how that increased the agency of humans?*

Mathias answered: *I certainly remember the part about opposition. That's one of the troubling aspects about Earth life. I should probably read The Word again, though, to refresh myself on just how that works.*

Pausing for a moment, Laura meditated upon the words of Lehi. Then she thought transmitted: *Let me quote from some of Lehi's text in the part of the History that he wrote for his son Jacob:*

> *For it must needs be, that there is an opposition in all things. If not so, my first-born in the wilderness, righteousness could not be brought to pass, neither wickedness, neither holiness nor misery, neither good nor bad. Wherefore, all things must needs be a compound in one; wherefore, if it should be one body it must needs remain as dead, having no life neither death, nor corruption nor incorruption, happiness nor misery, neither sense nor insensibility. . . .*

Mathias smiled as Laura gave her quotation. He knew that she could readily quote the entire passage, rather than a portion of it. He transmitted: *That's one of the things that I love about you, Laura, your knowledge of The Word, and your understanding of The Plan. Everything seems so clear to you—and when I listen to you it seems more understandable to me, also. If I just were not so deficient. . . . I know that my faith is weak, and I am too easily discouraged. If only I didn't have so many doubts. . . .*

You're not deficient, Mathias; you're a wonderful, vibrant, intelligent spirit, and I love you. If you didn't go to Earth with me I don't know what I'd do. In that regard, I've something important to tell you. But, could we speak orally, as Teacher Gallexus told us to do?

"If you wish to speak, orally, of course we can. It seems so clumsy, though, and it's much harder to understand the words than it is to understand transmitted thoughts. On Krasak-3 they express themselves with thoughts, just as we do here." Mathias smiled as he made this last point, and he wondered what Laura's reaction would be to this point.

Laura smiled in return and said: "Yes, and Gallexus told us that one of the reasons people could not, normally, thought transmit on Earth was to protect agency. If people can't know what another person is thinking, then those who are so inclined may lie, cheat, or deceive without being easily discovered. Those who choose to follow Satan, therefore, may freely do so without others knowing their true motivation."

"What a delightful place," Mathias said sarcastically. They both laughed. Then, becoming serious, Mathias asked, "What is it that you have to tell me, Laura?"

Mathias could feel the excitement in Laura as she responded: "Do you remember when Gallexus asked me if I'd take another assignment?"

"Yes."

"Actually, it was not another assignment from Gallexus, it was a new calling that Brother Brigham extended."

"Brother Brigham?"

"Yes. He explained that the Son wanted me to take the Earthly calling of being a mother of a prophet. In that calling my birth would be through the Earthly line of Brother Parley and Sister Thankful."

Mathias desperately tried to shield his thoughts and emotions from Laura. The mother of a prophet! She was surely ready for this enormous calling, but as for himself? . . . How could he ever be the father of a prophet? And the risks. . . . Did Laura really understand the risks?

Shielding his thoughts with difficulty, Mathias said: "What a wonderful opportunity for you, Laura. I'm thrilled for you."

"It's a wonderful opportunity, but for both of us, not just me."

"How so?"

"We can still go ahead with our plans, the ones we made one-thousand annuals ago, to work together and choose common goals—and to go to Earth together. If we maintain the proper spirit we can find each other on Earth and become eternal companions. And we can be parents of a prophet."

"I don't know, Laura. It all seems so out-of-reach, so difficult. There are so many things that could go wrong. The very principle that you say is so important to us, agency, could destroy everything that we planned for."

Hiding her emotions was difficult for Laura, but she didn't want Mathias to know her real feelings. She loved him immensely, but if he couldn't respond to her calling, then what? . . . There were things that were even more important than their love—or were there? For a brief moment Laura felt some doubt about herself.

Carefully choosing her words, Laura said: "It's true that agency can work against us as well as for us. But if we have faith, and trust in the Son, our prayers *will* be answered. I know they will. My feelings on really important matters have never failed me."

Mathias grinned wryly as he thought of the many times Laura had told him of her feelings about some future event, and had most often been right. He wondered why he was not similarly blessed. He squelched his thoughts and asked timidly: "What is it you want me to do?"

"It's more a question of what *you* want to do, Mathias. If you still want us to go ahead with our original plan, to work together for an Earth mission, then you need to take some steps toward that end. If, on the other hand, you want to take some other course of action, such as going to Krasak-3, then you need to tell me so that I can make other plans."

Mathias was shocked at Laura's response. In the past she had attempted to strengthen his resolve to proceed with difficult issues, but here . . . where it counted the most. It appeared that he would have to come to a decision solely from his own knowledge and faith. He wondered, was his faith strong enough?

"I wish I were sure of what I wanted to do, Laura. My feelings for you haven't changed; I love you with everything in me, and I want to stay with you. If only we could have gone to Krasak-3 together—but with your new calling I see that's not possible. So, I just don't know . . ."

"Why don't you spend several Quiets in meditation and prayer, and talk to your two teachers, Gallexus from Earth and Uval from Krasak-3? They should be able to help you decide. Then let me know about your decision. I'll be busy on the assignments Brother Brigham gave me to prepare myself for Earth."

"All right, Laura, I'll do as you suggest. But, please don't make any alternate plans with anyone else until I have a chance to get my thoughts together. Just remember that I love you more than anything else."

"I'll remember, Mathias, and I love you. May the Spirit be with you."

"And may the Spirit be with you, Laura."

Chapter 4

HOW DOES BIRTH WORK?

Our birth is but a sleep and a forgetting:
The soul that rises with us, our life's star,
Hath had elsewhere its setting,
And cometh from afar:
Not in entire forgetfulness,
And not in utter nakedness,
But trailing clouds of glory do we come
From God, who is our home. . . . [1]

Meeting with Brother Parley and Sister Thankful, Laura was discussing some of the aspects of the training for her Earthly calling. Brother Parley was speaking: "We were fortunate that the Son chose our family to have this special calling, and we'll be pleased to have you join our Earthly family tree. The people who've been called to be your parents have two small boys, and the family lives in the relatively small town of Price, Utah, in the United States of America. The United States, as you know, is the strongest and most free country on Earth. Utah is where Brother Brigham led the saints when he was a prophet during his birth-life on Earth."

"Do the Earthlings in your family tree know that they were chosen to be my parents?" asked Laura.

---

1 Wordsworth, William, 1770-1850, *Ode, Intimations of Immortality from Recollections of Early Childhood*, st. 5, 1807.

"Not now. They accepted the calling before they were born, just as you have, but they've forgotten their premortal commitments. Some help may be needed from us, since they're struggling with a problem. It should not . . ."

Thankful interrupted Parley: "The family's a lovely one, Laura. There's much love, and they desperately want more children. Your father-select is Alma Pratt, and he's the LDS Bishop of the Price 10th Ward. Janis, his wife, and your mother-select is a descendant of Brother Brigham. She's the stake family history representative and the ward organist. Their two children are Jeremy, who's eight years old, and Sherman, who's four years old."

Thankful continued, "The problem that Parley spoke of involves a chronic illness that Janis has—she's a diabetic. Currently the diabetes is under control. When Janis had her last child, though, the doctor told her that she should never have another child. He suggested that she have a minor operation that would prevent her from ever having a child again, and her husband urged her to do it, but she decided against the operation."

"Then she can still have me?"

Parley responded: "Yes, but with considerable risk to her own health. What's been encouraging, though, is her attitude. When her husband wanted her to have the operation to stop having children, she told him that she'd rather leave it in the Lord's care. She assured Alma that she'd know what the Lord wanted for her when the time came. They both want more children, but Alma is afraid for his wife's health. They've tried, unsuccessfully, to get a child by adoption."

"May I see them?"

Parley smiled. "Of course you may. In fact, we'll shortly make a trip to Earth, since they need your encouragement—and they need an answer to some of their prayers. But you should know more about them first. What ages would you wish to see them as?"

Laura gave thought before she answered Brother Parley. She certainly wanted to see her future parents as they now were, but she was also curious about their childhood. Were they raised in happy homes, and did this have an effect on how they turned out? Were their parents (her grandparents to be) loving people? Also, was their courtship an exciting one—did they remember each other from their previous spiritual estate?

"Let's first see them as children, then as young adults, and finally, in a recent experience. That should give me a feeling for my future family."

Feeling at peace with herself, Laura gazed around the room in the Library that she and the Pratts were occupying. There was a slight glow from the energy field that filled the room, and soft music caressed her spirit. From experience with Earth-time visions she understood the need for relaxation, so she relaxed further and concentrated on what she knew of the Pratts. Suddenly, as though she were transported to another place and another time, she saw, in three dimensions and in color, a small boy attempting to mount a pony. The pony was bare-back, and the boy had led the pony to a fence so that he could climb on its back. Laura could smell the country air, and she could feel the excitement of the boy as he maneuvered the pony.

Standing somewhat to the side of the corral was a tall man dressed in blue coveralls. He was speaking: "Go easy with the bridle, Alma. The pony is just as nervous as you are, so let him know that you're his friend. Give him another sugar."

Alma did as he was told, then asked: "Do you think that Spot likes me Dad?"

The tall man answered: "I'm sure he does, Alma, with all the sugar you've given him. He's just a little nervous, is all. Now slowly climb the fence, holding him close to it. Then slip your leg over his back, ease yourself onto his back, and hold the halter gently."

Feeling the excitement, mixed with fear, of the boy, Laura watched. She could also feel the pride—and great love—of the father for the boy. As she watched, Alma did as he was told. The pony stood quietly while the boy mounted him. Looking back at Alma, for a moment, the pony then focused on the tall man and walked slowly toward him.

"Look, Dad, I did it," the boy proudly proclaimed. Laura felt of his exhilaration, and this time there was no fear.

The entire scene was completed in a mere moment, but the feelings and impressions that Laura had received lasted. She knew instantly, for example, of the immense and unqualified love that the father had for the boy. In return, she could feel the near worship of the boy for his father.

While she was pondering what she had just seen, she found herself as the part of a different experience. Examining her surroundings, she observed that she was in a small room with three other people. One was a middle-aged man in a white coat, and sitting in chairs across from him were a young woman and a girl. The girl had large brown eyes, as did her mother sitting next to her, and Laura understood that the girl was nine years old. The man was talking.

"Tests of your daughter's condition were conclusive, Mrs. Miller. Janis has juvenile diabetes. There's no known cure for it, but fortunately, with proper treatment, and with diet and exercise, she should be able to live a nearly normal life."

Experiencing a surge of fear from the mother, Laura watched as the mother asked: "What do you mean, Dr. Tanner, *nearly* normal?"

"She can go to school and play, as normal children do, but she must take her insulin shots two or three times daily—we'll have to experiment with that to know just what it takes to control her blood sugar—and she'll have to learn to avoid sugar. That is, natural sugar in all its food forms—no candy, no cake, no cookies, no soda pop, no ice cream—at least none of those foods that are prepared with natural sugar. Those that use artificial sweeteners are okay."

"Oh my, that sounds very restrictive."

"It is when you first go on the diet, and it can be traumatic for the youngsters when they start the shots. The most important part of controlling diabetes is to become knowledgeable about the disease. Both you and Janis should become expert in what's good for her and what is not. I have a pamphlet, here, put out by the American Diabetes Association that's excellent. You should read it and teach Janis what's in it. We can discuss it on your next visit. In the meantime the nurse will start Janis on her shots. Within a month, you and she should be giving the shots yourselves."

Doctor Tanner paused to watch his patient, and Laura could feel of his concern. Looking at Janis, Laura saw tears, and she felt of the little girl's fear and confusion. Bravely biting her lip to keep from crying, Janis asked: "Will I be okay, Mommy?"

Norma Miller gathered her daughter in her arms and said: "Of course you're going to be okay, Darling. We're fortunate that Dr. Tanner was able to find out what was making you sick. You remember how Daddy blessed you that we'd find out what was wrong so we could make you better. Now you won't feel so weak and tired all the time, and you won't frighten Mommy and Daddy by going unconscious. We'll just have to learn what's good for you so you'll feel well all of the time. You'd like that, wouldn't you?"

Janis wiped the tears from her eyes and smiled at her mother. She responded, simply: "Yes, Mommy." Observing this event with some emotion, Laura was washed by a feeling of complete trust and love that was emitted from the little girl as she kissed her mother.

The scene faded from view and Laura struggled to control her emotions as she seemed to be transported into the next experience. There was an enormous crowd in a stadium, and they all appeared to be shouting at once. Laura's attention was drawn to a young woman, whom she knew to be Janis, and to the young woman's companion, Alma. Janis had long dark hair, a tan from time spent in the Phoenix sun, a laughing demeanor, and large brown eyes that were focussed on Alma.

Feeling of Janis's amusement at Alma's actions, Laura paused to watch him. He was jumping up and down and shouting: "They did it. Did you see that pass? What a game—it will go down in history as one of the great football games of all time. Do you understand what that means? We were down by 20 points with just four minutes left, and we won. Wow!"

"Yes, Alma, I know what that means. It means that we had an exciting time, at a terrific football game, and it means that I'm engaged to a most wonderful man."

Laura could sense that Alma was filled with love for the beautiful creature beside him. His feelings told Laura that he was still in shock that Janis had accepted his proposal of marriage on the previous evening. Laura wondered if her experience with courtship and marriage—hopefully to Mathias—would create feelings in her as powerful as the ones she now felt from her parents-select.

Alma then said: "I love you, Brown Eyes. What a marvelous day."

Watching the crowd disperse, Laura felt herself drawn to these two young people. The exuberance of life spilled from them to her, and she understood the depth of the love that they felt for each other. There was an eager anticipation for all that life has to offer, and Laura let her spirit embrace their spirits as she shared this moment of happiness.

The next vision opened, and Laura observed the Pratt family kneeling at a bedside as they offered their morning prayer. The oldest boy, Jeremy, was acting as voice. " . . . And we thank thee, Father in Heaven, that we're able to live in this nice house, and in this awesome valley. We're grateful that Grandma Norma was able to visit us, and we pray that she'll be protected on her trip back to Phoenix. Please bless Mom, so that she'll stay well, and help Mom and Dad so we can have another brother. . . ."

Watching the family offer their morning prayers, Laura observed the aura that surrounded them. The aura joined in an energy beam that was directed from them through the ceiling and toward Kolob. This truly was a good family, and she would do all that she could to help answer their prayers.

Upon completing the prayer, Jeremy jumped to his feet, and was ready to run out when his mother asked: "Are you sure that Heavenly Father wants us to have another boy, Jeremy? What if it's a girl?"

"Aw, it wouldn't be a girl, Mom. She couldn't help with the horses."

Janis laughed as her two bundles of energy bounded from the room. Janis's laughing face recorded itself in Laura's memory as Laura found herself again in the Library room with Brother Parley and Sister Thankful.

Thankful was laughing. "Aren't they a lovely family, Laura?"

"They surely are. I can hardly wait to join them. How serious is Janis's diabetes, though?"

"It's very serious, Laura," said Parley. "That's why Alma doesn't want Janis to have any more children. In fact, your birth could threaten her life."

"Should they have me, then?"

"As you remember, it was a calling that they accepted before their birth-life. But, if they choose not to, then the blessing will move to some other family," Parley responded.

"Could we view them in a future-vision?"

"Yes, but you should know that the usual most probable vision doesn't exist—there are two equally probable futures. Do you still want to see them?"

"Yes, I do."

Laura found herself in a hospital delivery room. Dressed in hospital clothes, and holding his wife's hand was Alma. He was saying: "One more push, Janis, and the baby will be here."

"That's right, Janis," confirmed the doctor, "I can see the head. Give one more push."

Feeling the exhaustion and the pain of Janis, Laura watched as Janis gave a mighty push and the baby, Laura, was born. What a thrill she felt as she observed her own birth.

"It's a girl," the doctor announced. Laura heard and felt the cry of joy that Janis emitted. The vision faded. . . .

Next, Laura observed Alma in an office. He was holding his head in his hands with his elbows on his knees. And he was crying. The doctor was sitting opposite from him at a desk.

"I'm terribly sorry, Alma, we did all that we could to save her. I wish there were something I could say or do that would ease your pain or bring Janis back, but . . ."

Alma didn't look up as his arms and shoulders shook uncontrollably. Laura felt the sobs of Alma as if they were coming from her. Then the vision faded and she was back in the Library.

Addressing Parley and Thankful, it was all that Laura could do to keep her emotions in check. "You say that these two futures are equally probable?"

"Yes. It's unusual, I know, but that's true," Parley responded.

"What is it that determines which future will occur?"

Parley smiled, thoughtfully. "There are thousands of events that have an impact on the future, Laura. Everything that happens affects everything else. There are such issues as how good her doctor is, whether he's too busy, or adequately trained to handle her case. What kind of blessing her husband gives her, and the children's prayers, are very important. Perhaps, most important, is whether or not she's accomplished all that she set out to do in her Earthly mission. And, yes, Satan can have an effect if the family allows him into their lives."

"But she could give up her life just to have me. That doesn't seem to be a good . . ."

Interrupting Laura, Parley said: "Earth life can sometimes be hard—the lessons aren't easy. But then, you're starting to think in terms of an Earthling. Death is often tragic from their perspective. You should remember, though, that, except in extremely rare circumstances, death is inevitable, not optional. The only real question is when it will occur, not whether it will occur.

"Viewed from our perspective, if the person has completed the mission they were assigned, Earthly death is a glorious event. Even the term *death* is a term that we don't usually use. As you know, we call it the fourth birth. It's just one of the five births we go through.

"Please explain the five births, again, Brother Parley."

"You're familiar with them, Laura. The first birth, you remember, was when we were born as spirit children to Elohim, the Father, and to our Heavenly Mother. That birth occurred when our spirits were created from our eternal intelligences—before the great war.

"For all those who sided with Jehovah in the great war, the second birth occurs when each individual goes to Earth, or some other planet, to receive a physical body. Those who sided with Lucifer never receive anything beyond the first birth. To borrow an Earthly term, death, for them, was permanent when they were cast out of Elohim's presence. To you, Laura, your second birth will occur when you're born on Earth with your spirit housed in a completely physical frame.

"The third birth occurs when each individual repents of his or her sins and is baptized by someone having the authority of Father to perform the ordinance. It is a planetary, physical ordinance involving complete immersion in water, and it must be performed in that environment, either directly, or vicariously. It signifies a new birth into the Son's church. Baptism is essential for entrance into the Father's kingdom.

"So, you see, baptism is the third birth. The fourth birth is the one we've been talking about when Earthly death occurs. It, just as with the other births, is, for those who successfully completed their missions, a marvelous happening accompanied by much joy and happiness. On the other hand, for those who followed Satan on Earth, their birth into the spiritual world truly is a death since they're cut off from Father's presence. They're consigned to spirit prison, hell, until the final resurrection. The fourth birth is, to them, and to those of us who view it, a disaster of unmitigated proportions—they'll live as spirits in the agony of forever missed opportunity.

"The final, and fifth birth occurs at the resurrection, and this is the most glorious event of all. Every spirit who's lived on a planetary system, whether or not they lived up to their potential, will eventually participate in this event. All will receive a new physical body with this birth, and this will be a body that can never be destroyed. The jubilation at having the spirit and physical body reunited will be beyond measure, especially for those who are inhabitants of the Celestial Kingdom with the Father and the Son.

"So, you see, Laura, the fourth birth, or Earthly death, is merely another step in The Plan, which provides for our progression on a path back to the Father and the Son. It doesn't have the negative connotation that Earthlings normally put on it. In fact, just the opposite is true, it provides new opportunity for growth— both for those on Earth, and for those in the spiritual realm."

"Now, Laura, have you seen enough in vision?" asked Parley. "Are you ready to join me in a trip to Earth to see, first-hand, your chosen family?"

"Yes, Brother Parley, I am."

Chapter 5

ANOTHER CHILD?

Know you what it is to be a child? . . . it is to believe in love, to believe in loveliness, to believe in belief; . . . it is to turn pumpkins into coaches, and mice into horses, lowness into loftiness, and nothing into everything. [1]

Driving to work for Alma Pratt with his companion, Jim Blair, was a pleasant experience. They usually left Price at 6:30 a.m. for the forty-minute drive to the Hunter power plant just below Castle Dale. During the drive they discussed work, or just as frequently, their duties in the Price 10th Ward.

It was a convenient arrangement. Alma was the Plant Manager for the Hunter Power Plant, and Jim was the Maintenance Superintendent. In the ward, Alma was Bishop, and Jim was the Executive Secretary. Their families were close, often taking picnics together in the nearby Wasatch Plateau west of Huntington.

With three children and a fourth on the way, Jim and Lori were fully occupied with the raising of their children. Alma and Janis, with their two children, wondered if they would ever have any more. This was much on Alma's mind as he asked Jim: "How's Lori's pregnancy going, Jim?"

"Oh, you know Lori, Alma. Nothing gets her down. Since we've been married, and all through her previous pregnancies, I can't remember when she was sick. She's always ready to go. As

---

1 Thompson, Francis, 1859-1907, *Shelley. In the Dublin Review*, July 1908.

busy as she is she still seems to have energy left over. If it were up to her we'd have a dozen kids—maybe we will." Jim laughed as he thought about it.

"You're so fortunate. Janis keeps pushing for another child, and it scares me to death."

"What does Doctor Lewis say?"

"He insists that we not have another child. He says that with Janis's diabetes he's not sure they could save either the child or Janis in a difficult pregnancy—and both of her pregnancies were difficult."

"I thought that her diabetes was under good control."

"It is now, and I'd like to keep it that way. Any little thing can set it off, though."

"Can't you get Janis to relax and just enjoy the children you have? Your two boys must be a handful."

Alma laughed as he thought of his boys. "They are a handful, Jim, and that's the argument I use on Janis. It used to be that she just smiled when I said our family was large enough, but lately she's really been pushing the idea of another child. I'm not sure what's gotten into her."

"You know women, Alma. When they get their mind set on something, it's difficult to change it."

"You're right, they're far less flexible than we are about most matters. I usually give Janis her way except on the really important issues, such as deer hunting, or a new pickup truck." Both men laughed.

Driving the rest of the way to work in silence, Jim and Alma were lost in their thoughts. Jim felt sympathy for Janis and Alma, but he knew there was not much he could do about it—except to offer his prayers on their behalf. An issue that bothered him more was the schedule for the maintenance of the Hunter 3 turbine coming up in a month. Jim wanted to have his crew do the work, without contract help, but he wasn't sure Alma would approve. He would talk to Alma later about it.

Thinking about Janis, Alma felt an immense happiness for the blessings that were his. His two boys and his fabulous wife, they were more than he deserved. His work kept him busy, and being bishop of the ward didn't leave him much personal time, but the joy he felt made it all worth while. If only Janis could be as satisfied as he was with the way things were.

Janis sometimes accused Alma of having little faith. Grinning to himself as he thought about it, he wondered what she thought it took to be bishop. He had as much faith as most active church-going men. . . . Maybe that was it. Women seemed to be more spiritual and to have more faith than men. Why was that?

It wasn't that he was oblivious to Janis's needs. He under-stood her desire to have another child. It was just that . . . she didn't seem to understand the danger. Not wanting to frighten her about the seriousness of her diabetes, Alma didn't talk about it often. Still, when Dr. Lewis explained the risks to both of them, it should have been clear to Janis that there was a real danger that she would not survive the birth of another child.

The thought of losing Janis was almost more than Alma could bear. The boys needed their mother, and Alma needed his wife. They were a family—an eternal family—and they needed to continue as a complete family until their missions were complete. Alma was sure that Janis's mission was not yet complete, but he didn't want to tempt fate by exposing her to unnecessary risks.

Rushing to get Jeremy and Sherman ready for school, Janis was trying to be finished before Lori picked her up for their 9:30 a.m. appointment at the stake family history center. Jim had picked Alma up for the ride to work promptly at six, and Janis knew that Lori would be on time—she always was. Janis wondered how Lori did it with all her children. Barely completing breakfast, Janis was taking her insulin shots when she heard Lori's honk in the driveway.

"Hi Janis. Did I rush you?" Lori asked as Janis breathlessly entered the car.

"No, I'm okay. It's just a hassle to get the boys ready for school. There's always something that they leave for the last minute, such as their homework."

"I know what you mean. My tribe is never ready for school, but they're always instantly ready for a ball game." Lori paused as Janis settled in the car. Then she commented: "When you phoned last night, you mentioned wanting to talk about something that was troubling you. What was it Janis?"

Having asked the question, Lori was immediately sorry that she had. Looking at Janis, she saw tears form in Janis's eyes and cascade down her cheeks.

"I'm sorry Lori," said Janis as she wiped away the tears. "I didn't mean to be such a baby. Whenever the subject comes up, it's all I can do . . ."

"That's okay, Janis. If there's anything I can do to help please let me know."

"Talking to you'll be a big help. I've talked to my Mom, and she feels a lot like Alma. I understand what they're saying, but I need to talk to someone who has a different perspective."

"What is it that's troubling you?"

"You know the difficulty I've had with my diabetes?"

"Yes, but I thought it was now under good control."

"It is, and that's the whole point."

"What do you mean?"

"I mean that my diabetes has been under excellent control for over a year now, and I should be able to . . ." Janis choked up and was unable to continue for a minute. "I'm sorry. What I meant to say was that by now I should be able to carry a baby full-term."

"Doesn't Alma agree with that?"

"No. He listens too much to Dr. Lewis, and all they can think about is the risk."

"What *is* the risk?"

"If you believe Dr. Lewis, my diabetes could get worse, and if that happened, I could . . . die."

Lori was quiet while she digested what Janis had told her. She was aware of Janis's desire for further children, of course, but this was the first time that she had heard Janis admit to the risks. She needed to consider what she said carefully so that Janis wouldn't misunderstand her. Janis was a good friend, and Lori wanted to support her, but to risk death? . . . Maybe she could just avoid further comment about the subject—just change the subject. No, she owed Janis more than that. She owed her the truth as Lori saw it.

"Death is a pretty serious risk, Janis."

"I know, but . . ."

"Have you considered what would happen to Alma and the boys if they lost you?"

"That's the argument that Alma uses, and yes I have considered it, but . . . but the feeling I have is . . ."

"What kind of feeling?"

"Well, you know how you mentioned the urgency you feel about performing genealogy work for Jim?"

"Yes, it really bugs me at times. I think *he* should get those feelings on his line, not me." Lori smiled to herself as she thought about it.

Janis continued: "For whatever reason I keep getting this feeling of urgency about another child. Sometimes I can't sleep at night because of it. It's an overwhelming feeling that I'm supposed to have another child."

"No doubt you've prayed about it?"

"My, yes. That seems to make the feelings even more intense."

"Have you asked Alma to give you a priesthood blessing?"

Janis was afraid Lori would ask her that question. How could she explain the relationship that existed between Alma and herself? Alma was such a physical, outdoor person. She was still surprised that he had been made bishop. There was no questioning his love for her and the children, but he was so silent on issues of this sort. Occasionally he would express his concern about the risks to her—as when they both met with Dr. Lewis—but mostly Alma seemed to keep such thoughts to himself.

Then there was another thing. Because of Alma's deeply felt reluctance for her to risk having another child, she was not sure that he could give her a proper blessing. How could she tell Lori of her doubts? . . .

Lori interrupted Janis's thoughts by asking, again: "Have you asked Alma for a blessing?"

"No. Actually, I'm afraid to. He's so prejudiced that I'm afraid of what he'll say."

"Shame on you, Janis. You know better than that."

"Maybe I do, but I'm still afraid to ask."

"Alma's love for you is firm, isn't it?"

"Of course."

"And he loves the children?"

"Yes, but . . ."

"Does he honor his priesthood?"

"Sure. I don't know any other men who are more faithful to their callings than my husband."

"With all those attributes, don't you think that he's entitled to the spirit of the Lord to guide him in a blessing?"

Janis's eyes filled with tears, and her lip began quivering. Fumbling for a Kleenex in her purse, she wiped her eyes. "You're right, Lori. My husband is a good man, and he is entitled to the spirit of the Lord."

"Well then?"

"What should I do?"

"Why not ask him for a specific blessing to know what you both should do?"

"Lori, thank you. Of course you're right. I guess I just needed somebody to tell me what I already knew.

Having completed dinner, Janis and Alma were sitting in the living room, reading, and the boys were in their room watching TV. Janis completed a silent prayer and then said: "Alma, would you do me a favor?"

"Sure, Babe. What can I do for you?"

"Would you give me a special priesthood blessing?"

Alma felt a surge of fear as he realized what Janis was asking of him. He loved her so . . . and he desperately wanted to shield her from hurt. How, without hurting her, could he tell her that they should not have any more children? Surely, she knew the risks?

All she was asking him, though, was to give her a blessing. There was nothing to fear from that, was there? He held and honored the Melchizedek Priesthood, and he knew of its power. What, then, was holding him up?

Alma was silent for a moment. Then he asked: "What do you want the blessing for?"

"I'd like you to bless me so that I might know whether I should have another child or not."

"Well, I . . ."

It was all Janis could do to keep from crying as she sensed Alma's resistance. She knew that he didn't like her to show emotion when they were discussing issues such as this, but really! Was she asking so much of him?

"Will you give me the blessing, or not?"

"Of course I will, Janis. It's just that you took me by surprise. Would you like the blessing now?"

"Yes, as soon as the boys are in bed."

❦   ❦   ❦   ❦

Sitting in the chair with Alma's hands on her head, Janis waited. Then the words came:

Janis Young Pratt, by the authority of the Melchizedek Priesthood, which I hold, I place my hands on your head and give you a blessing.

I bless you, first, that you might know that you are a choice daughter of our Father in Heaven, and He is pleased with you. He hears your prayers and knows of the secret desires of your heart.

You have many blessings—a loving husband and two wonderful children—and these blessings are of an eternal nature.

Now, as to your specific request, to know whether you should have another child, please know, dear sister, that you have the power to call upon Father and receive an answer. In response to your prayer you will have a peaceful reassurance concerning the course of action you should take.

Be further assured that, if the answer is affirmative, you will have the health and strength to carry the child to the full term. Also, be assured that when you receive your answer and tell it to your husband, he will . . .

Alma was unable to continue the blessing for a moment. Upon recovering his composure, he continued.

. . . your husband will be fully supportive of your decision. Know that your husband and children love you dearly, and they want only what's best for you. You'll understand, in time . . .

There was much more to the blessing, but these were the words that burned into Janis's memory. She'd remember them for all time.

Upon completion of the blessing, Janis and Alma had a tearful, and long, embrace. When Janis could speak, she said: "Thank you, dear, darling Alma. That was a marvelous blessing; it means more to me than you can imagine. I love you so much."

"And I love you, also, dearest. More than life itself."

Retiring to their bedroom shortly thereafter, both Alma and Janis spent considerable time on their knees before they got in bed. Falling asleep in each other's arms was a not uncommon experience, but this night especially, they shared in a serene tranquility that was rare.

Awakened from a sound sleep, Alma looked at the clock. It was 3:20 a.m. He was sure he'd heard something. Then he heard it again, his name as though muttered in a muffled sob. It was Janis, and she was crying.

Turning on the light, Alma asked: "What is it Janis, why are you crying?"

Between sobs, Janis managed to say: "She was here, Alma. She was here—I saw her."

"Who was here? What're you talking about?"

"It was our daughter. I saw our daughter."

Alma was silent for a long moment. Then, taking Janis in his arms to still her alternate sobs and laughter he said: "Tell me what happened."

"It was the most amazing thing. I was sleeping, and . . . no, I'd awakened. Something strange was happening, and I could feel a presence. Suddenly, as I was looking around the room, it started getting light."

"What started getting light?"

"The room. At first it was just a hint of light. Then it got brighter and brighter, and there she was, in the midst of the light. In fact, she seemed to be a part of the light, sort of translucent. The whole effect was transcendentally beautiful."

Janis was silent for awhile. She felt an explosion of joy as she lay in Alma's arms. The peace that enveloped her was beyond belief, beyond ecstasy. She had been privileged to glimpse eternity—where angels and her daughter dwelt—and she would never forget what she had seen and felt.

Alma interrupted Janis's reverie with a question. "What did she look like?"

"She was tall, and she had on a long flowing white gown with a golden belt. There were no shoes or slippers on her feet, and she seemed to be standing in the air, just at the foot of our bed. Her hair was long, and it was a bright red color, more red than your mother's."

"Was she a child?"

"No. She appeared as a young woman, perhaps in her early twenties."

"Did she say anything?"

"Not at first. There was the most loving smile on her face that I've ever seen. Then she said . . . it was not anything that she spoke with her mouth. Rather it came from her mind to mine. I could hear her voice in my mind. And all she said was: "Mother."

Janis began to cry again, and Alma held her until she quieted. She continued: "While she was present there was the most peaceful, wonderful feeling. I felt that everything would be all right. No matter what happened, I felt . . ."

"I know," Alma said with a husky voice, "I feel it too."

"You do? Now?"

"Yes."

"What do you think of it all?"

What did he think of it? How could he answer that without crying? And men never cried—at least that was what Alma had believed to this point in his life. Now, he wasn't so sure. He was overwhelmed with a feeling of peace—and of an ethereal presence that seemed to permeate the room.

Janis repeated her question: "What do you think of my experience?"

With difficulty, Alma answered: "I think you got the answer to your prayer."

Chapter 6

MORE ABOUT EARTH

Viewed from the distance of the moon, the astonishing thing about the earth . . . is that it is alive. . . . Aloft, floating free beneath the moist, gleaming membrane of bright blue sky, is the rising earth, the only exuberant thing in this part of the cosmos. . . . It has the organized, self-contained look of a live creature, full of information, marvelously skilled in handling the sun. [1]

Going back to Earth-school was hard for Mathias, but he decided if he wanted to see Laura again he would, at least, have to attend the class. He could decide later whether or not he would go to Earth. He still liked the idea of the easier life associated with Krasak-3, but that choice led away from Laura, and at least for now, he could not make that choice.

Neither could he, at this point in his understanding, commit unequivocally to a hard life on Earth. The idea of finding Laura after birth, when their memory of a previous life had been completely obliterated, was almost overwhelming. It was true that he would have prayer, and there would be the prompting of helping angels, but there would be no direct communication with those from the spirit realm—at least under most circumstances. The risks seemed enormous.

---

1 Thomas, Lewis, 1913- , *The Lives of a Cell—The World's Biggest Membrane*, 1974.

64

Completing his Quiet, Mathias closed with a prayer, then willed himself to the Library where this rotation's class would be held. The students were just assembling when Mathias entered the classroom. Teacher Gallexus smiled at him and transmitted a welcome. Most of the students were different from those he remembered.

Gallexus began speaking orally. "This learning session will cover the following subjects: Caring for your body, and how Satan will seek to destroy you. Both subjects will be considered in the context of agency. You may ask any questions that you wish, but please speak orally since you'll have to speak in that manner when you're on Earth.

"As we learned in an earlier session, your physical body will be made of the basic building blocks of matter. The life force for your body will be provided by your spirit, and birth-life will begin when your spirit enters your physical body while it's still in your mother's womb. From that point on your entire existence will depend upon how well your body is cared for, either by others while you're a helpless infant, or by yourself as you get old enough and learn what's good for you and what's not." Gallexus sensed a question from one of the students. "Yes, Renfru?"

"In The Word, isn't there something about taking care of your body?"

"There's much that's been written by the prophets about our bodies. There is, of course, the portion of The Word from the Doctrine and Covenants that's called 'The Word of Wisdom.' It specifically instructs people that they should not drink strong drinks, such as coffee or tea, or drinks containing alcohol, and they shouldn't use tobacco, as humans are prone to do. It also instructs us that fruits and grains are to be used for food, as is flesh from beasts and fowls, in moderation."

"Do you mean that we will eat other living things?" Zaneth asked.

"Yes. That'll be necessary so that you can get the essential proteins, carbohydrates, vitamins, minerals and other substances to stay alive. These foods won't be alive when you eat them, of course. Fruits, vegetables and grains will have been harvested (picked), and animals will have been killed and processed."

Zaneth looked distressed. "How disgusting," she said.

Reading the thoughts of those in the class, Teacher Gallexus detected that others felt as Zaneth did. He smiled as he thought back on his own experience on Earth. Then he said: "Actually, you'll find that the experience of eating can be a very pleasant sensation. When the food is properly prepared and seasoned, with appetizing herbs and spices, it's very attractive to humans. This is one of the pleasant, and necessary, Earthly experiences.

"Have any of you seen a spirit eat?" Gallexus asked.

Mathias signalled that he had. Gallexus said: "Tell us about it Mathias."

"I saw a superior being, a resurrected one, give another spirit an apple."

"Was the one that got the apple also resurrected?"

"I don't know."

"It could have been either way. You can eat in this sphere, because you have all the spiritual body parts that you'll have on Earth. When that occurs it's usually for teaching purposes, since your primary energy is received from the Father and the Son.

"Eating food will teach you several important lessons. You'll feel hunger and thirst if you don't adequately refresh yourselves with food and drink, and those feelings of hunger and thirst can become urgent necessities. You'll thus quickly learn that, in order to survive, there's a necessity for constant nourishment. And just as your physical body will need constant nourishment from food and drink, your spiritual body will also need constant nourishment. Let me ask you, how may this spiritual nourishment be obtained on Earth?"

Responding hesitatingly, Mathias said: "By reading the Word, and by prayer."

"That's correct, Mathias, and another way is by listening to living prophets.

"We've already discussed how Satan can influence people to put harmful products into their bodies. His greatest power, however, comes through what he and his followers manage to put into peoples' minds. He does this in many subtle ways. Some of the more effective means are through the major communication sources on Earth: the written word, television, radio and movies. These sources are used by many to entertain themselves—a method of amusement that requires little effort. Satan influences men and women who create the entertainment sources to pollute them with messages that are contrary to The Word."

"How does he do that?" asked Zaneth.

"Let me answer that question by asking you, aside from life itself and the physical bodies that you'll get when you go to Earth, what's the most precious *new* gift that the Father and the Son will give you when you go there? As a hint, it's a gift that you don't now have, nor have you ever possessed it."

The class was silent for a period. Then Mathias responded: "Could it be the ability to create new life—to have children?"

"Good for you Mathias. Yes, the ability to create new life allows you to share one of the gifts of godhood. It's a tremendous blessing, and it's a probationary gift."

"I don't understand how it's probationary, Teacher Gallexus. What does that mean?" asked Renfru.

"It means that it's a transitory gift if it isn't treated properly."

"You mentioned Satan, Teacher Gallexus. What has he got to do with this gift?" asked Zaneth.

"That's an excellent question, Zaneth, and it goes directly to the issue of the transitory nature of the gift. Let me answer your question by directing a few questions to you. First, tell me if you can, how Father and the Son would like us to use this gift?"

Zaneth smiled. "That's an easy question to answer. The gift of life creation is to be used only within the sanctity of marriage."

"And if it's not used in marriage?"

"Then it's considered a sexual sin—probably the worst sin on Earth except for the shedding of innocent blood."

"Good, Zaneth. So, from Satan's point of view, how might he seek to frustrate the Father and the Son's Plan concerning this particular commandment?"

"I suppose, by attempting to persuade Earthlings that it's not wrong to use that gift outside of marriage."

"Exactly. And how might he do that?"

"I'm not sure, since it seems so obviously against The Word."

"That's true. But let's grant that many individuals don't necessarily believe The Word. How might he persuade them?"

Zaneth puzzled the question for a moment. Then she said: "We know that the bodies we'll receive have certain natural desires—and needs—built into them, such as the need for nourishment and rest, and the need to avoid pain. I assume that the same is true of the desire to create children. That must be a natural trait that results in pleasurable sensations. Satan could use that trait for his own purposes by persuading Earthlings that it may be used for their selfish pleasure—outside of marriage."

"You're more right than you know, Zaneth. How might he do that?"

Zaneth was silent for a period, and Mathias signalled a thought. "Yes, Mathias," said Gallexus.

"You mentioned how Satan and his followers try to influence those who create the entertainment and information media on Earth. Does that have an effect on how people behave sexually?"

"It does, indeed, Mathias. Supposedly wise writers, artists, actors and musicians create television and theater productions that glamorize—make attractive—the very thing that The Word says that we shouldn't do. The artists and creators of these shows depict sexual activities as having no moral consequence—what The Word or the prophets say is irrelevant to modern living, they say. They argue that consenting adults should be able to make their own choices, as long as it doesn't hurt others."

"But it does hurt others, doesn't it?" asked Xelee.

"Of course it does," continued Gallexus. "Terrible diseases are transmitted, children are born without fathers to care for them, and the entire moral fabric of Earth is hurt—exactly what Satan wants. In fact, the worst consequences are spiritual in nature, leading to a permanent loss of many spiritual gifts. One of the more insidious practices that has grown out of the decaying moral fibre is the termination of birth by physically aborting—destroying—babies in their mother's wombs."

Gallexus could feel the stunned horror of the class. There was silence for a time. Zaneth broke the silence. "Do you mean that they kill the babies?"

"Yes. The practice is condoned by much of society on Earth, and it's done to relieve mothers and fathers of the inconvenience of having an unwanted child. Abortion is presented as the right of the mother to exercise her choice concerning how she uses her body. There are, of course, legitimate reasons for terminating a pregnancy—such as saving the life of the mother—but the abortion practice goes far beyond anything Father would accept."

"Won't these sexual perversions and abortion practices bring down the judgment of Father and the Son?" asked Mathias.

"Ultimately it will. But in order for agency to persist, those perverted actions inspired by Satan will be allowed to continue. Earthlings must be free to choose their own way through life. The irony of their position, however, is that the very thing many of them treasure most—freedom of sexual activity—will be lost because of the misuse of this freedom. This is the probationary nature of the creative gift I previously spoke about."

"They will lose it when they leave the Earth. Is that correct?" asked Mathias.

"You're right, Mathias. The ability to have children in the life to come is restricted to those who inherit the Celestial Kingdom. All others will have a glory that will be pleasing to them, commensurate with how they lived on Earth, but it won't include the gift of life creation. That will be lost forever."

"Isn't that true of many of the freedoms that we'll have on Earth?" asked Xelee. "Depending on how we use our free choice, we may or may not have that choice when we return to Father?"

"Precisely correct, Xelee. Many Earthlings, for example, are attracted to riches—money, gold, jewels, material possessions—and if these possessions are used selfishly they will be lost forever. Those who use their possessions to help others, on the other hand, will find riches beyond measure in the life to come. Similarly for those who seek after power, and misuse it, that gift will be lost forever when they leave Earth.

"Satan's success, though temporary, is remarkable. He uses The Plan's allowance of free choice to tempt Earthlings by means of avarice, greed, lust, envy, jealousy, fear, anger, covetousness, pride, arrogance and promises of power. The Father and the Son also use The Plan's allowance of free choice to persuade Earthlings by means of love, compassion, charity, sympathy, forgiveness, grace, peace, mercy, harmony, prayer, The Word, prophets, the Holy Ghost, and the spirit of the Son. As each of you goes to Earth you'll have the opportunity to exercise your free choice through these various options. How you choose will determine your ultimate position in eternity."

Mathias interjected: "It's too bad, Gallexus, that we won't be able to remember what you just told us when we go to Earth. That would help us considerably."

The class laughed. Gallexus smiled and said: "Not really, Mathias. It would actually reduce your freedom of choice, and consequently your ultimate growth would be retarded. Sort of like what happens on Krasak-3." He smiled again as he felt Mathias's reaction to his comment about Krasak-3.

"That will be enough for this teaching session. Some of you may get an opportunity to see Satan's handiwork first-hand through visions or through trips to Earth. If you do, remember how agency works within the context of The Plan.

Chapter 7

A VISIT TO HELL

Him the Almighty Power
Hurl'd headlong flaming from th' Ethereal Sky . . .
To bottomless perdition, there to dwell
In Adamantine Chains and penal Fire, . . .
A Dungeon horrible, on all sides round
As one great Furnace flam'd, yet from those flames
No light, but rather darkness visible
Serv'd only to discover sights of woe,
Regions of sorrow, doleful shades, where peace
And rest can never dwell, hope never comes . . . [1]

Standing atop Mount Isaiah, Mathias was thrilled by the sight. A mosaic of changing colors drifted through the Valley of the Son in response to the gentle puffs of clouds sailing across the pale pink sky. Knowing that this was one of the favorite places of Laura, Mathias had transmitted a message to her that he would meet her here. Her earlier thought-message to him, that she wanted to visit with him, had given Mathias new hope.

Contemplating the marvelous spirit that Laura was, Mathias wondered why she continued to associate with him. His progress, he knew, was much less than hers—actually, he acted as a hindrance to her rapid growth. He did not want to slow her

---

1 Milton, John, 1608-1674, *Paradise Lost*, 1677, Book I, lines 44, 47, 61-66.

growth, and yet . . . he needed a little more information before he committed unequivocally to Earth.

Mathias's thoughts of Laura were interrupted by the appearance of a brilliantly glowing spirit. Feelings of love and peace emanated from the glowing form. It was Laura.

Recovering from his surprise, Mathias thought transmitted: *Laura, your aura is so bright. What happened?*

Smiling at the confused spirit before her, Laura expressed her devotion to him. Then she said: "Mathias, I have wonderful things to tell you. Brother Parley has taught me so much."

"Brother Parley?"

"Yes. My birth will be through the descendants of Brother Parley and Sister Thankful. . . . Mathias, I saw her. I saw my mother. It was a remarkable experience, and she is a magnificent being."

"You're a magnificent being, Laura, but how did you see your mother? Was it a vision?"

"No. Brother Parley took me on a trip to Earth, and I was able to be with her. My feelings during the visit were beyond expression—and she saw me."

"She saw you?"

"Yes. She had prayed to know what she should do about my birth, and her faith was great. Because of her prayer and her faith I was able to show myself to her. The intensity of our love for each other was as strong as the love we feel here for superior beings."

"So, will you be going to Earth soon?"

"I'm not sure. It may be a while yet. My mother-select has some severe physical problems and she may have trouble getting pregnant.

"That wasn't why I wanted to see you, though, Mathias. I have a present for you, and a request."

"A present?"

"Yes. I brought back a rock from Earth." Laura held a dark-brown irregularly-shaped object in her hand. She presented it to Mathias.

Reaching for the rock, Mathias was surprised to see it pass through his reaching hand. Laughing at his surprise, Laura caught the falling rock.

"How'd you do that?" he asked.

"Through the power of The Word—Brother Parley taught me. The physical materials of Earth are more dense than here, and our spirit bodies normally pass through those materials, just as yours did. By exercising strong faith, however, and by using The Word we can exert control over the materials. Brother Parley said that visiting spirits on Earth sometimes find it necessary to intrude into the physical world of the Earthlings. So he taught me how to do it."

Mathias smiled. "Well, you'll have to keep my present until I can learn how to do it. You mentioned a request, though. What's the request?"

"Brother Parley is arranging another trip to Earth, and he suggested that you might want to come along. The three of us would go together. We'd be able to see, directly, how things on Earth work. A major part of the trip would be spent in observing Satan's handiwork among Earthlings."

"That's interesting. Teacher Gallexus said that some of the class members might get an opportunity to see how Satan did his work on Earth. I never thought it would be me."

"So, you'll go?"

"Yes. When I restarted Earth classes I decided to do whatever the Teacher recommended. Besides, that way I'll be with you."

Laura smiled and extended her love. She was elated with Mathias's more positive attitude. His willingness to undergo experiences that she knew were difficult for him spoke well of their possible future life together.

Watching Kolob-1 get smaller as they accelerated through space, Mathias was astonished at how easy it was. Brother Parley and Laura were on either side of him, and the stars of the Elohim

Galaxy whipped by with increasing speed until they were merely flashes of light.

Suddenly Mathias found himself over a valley with mountains on one side and strangely colored desert-type landscape in the valley. There were mesas and cliffs of brilliant red, orange and yellow colors, and there was a winding river that had cut a deep chasm in the canyon floor. A moderate-sized city was nestled against the mountains.

Interrupting Mathias's thoughts, Laura transmitted: *We're coming to the town of Price in Utah, Mathias. That's where my mother-select lives. See, that white house with the blue-trim is her house.*

The three spirits entered the house through the ceiling, and they found themselves in a small living room watching a young mother talking to a small, but husky boy. *That's her, Mathias,* excitedly transmitted Laura. *That's Janis, my mother-select.*

Watching the lovely lady that Laura had drawn his attention to, Mathias observed that an aura surrounded Janis's physical body. Similarly, the boy had an aura around him. The auras were not as bright as the ones surrounding Laura or Brother Parley, but they were nearly as bright as Mathias's aura.

Janis was saying: ". . . it may be some time, yet, Jeremy, but, yes, your father and I believe we should have another child—a beautiful baby girl."

"But, Mom," the boy was saying, "what makes you so sure it'll be a girl? She couldn't help with the stable."

Janis laughed a joyful, lilting laugh that penetrated Laura's spirit and filled her with a feeling of bliss.

"Jeremy," Janis said, "I'm not sure that Heavenly Father considers the ability to clean the stable as the most important reason we should have a child."

Laura could have stayed forever watching the mother and son. During the experience she felt of Mathias's amazement—and of his love—for the people they were witnessing. She could tell that, by seeing first-hand her mother-select, he was gaining a much better appreciation for the joys and opportunities of Earth life. And she knew that he could feel Laura's thrill at the prospect of joining this wonderful family.

Interjecting into Laura's thoughts, Brother Parley transmitted: *We must leave. Our main purpose in visiting Earth was to show you how Satan influences people.*

Following Brother Parley seemed to be a matter of wishing yourself to be with him. It was similar to the experience of traveling on Kolob-1, except, of course, the surroundings were different. It was not as colorful as Kolob-1, and the feelings of life and joy were not as pronounced. There seemed to be a contrary feeling in the atmosphere. Mathias was not sure what it meant, but he continued to stay close to Brother Parley and Laura.

Looming in the distance was a large city in the midst of the desert. The Sun-star was setting on the western horizon, and the city was blanketed with many lights, some of them blinking garishly into the darkening sky. The entire scene seemed a vulgar and gaudy display to Mathias, with clashing lights competing for attention from adjacent structures. It was not at all like the cities of Kolob-1, which were also bathed in light, but with a blended ethereal light which calmed the spirit. This light had a disturbing effect on the spirit.

Brother Parley led them to the outskirts of the city where a smaller building stood with many white lights on an overhanging marquee. Displayed on the front of the marquee in blinking red lights was the sign: *GIRLS—GIRLS—GIRLS.*

Ignoring the sign, Brother Parley directed them through a nearby wall. Entering a smoke-filled and crowded room, Mathias's attention was drawn to an elevated platform where two young women, dressed in very little, were undulating to the beat of an extremely loud rhythmic sound.

Brother Parley transmitted: *That loud rhythmic noise you hear is called music by Earthlings.*

Mathias could scarcely believe that this discordant and overwhelming noise would be called music. On Kolob-1 music uplifted the spirit with the soft melodies from inspired composers. There was nothing uplifting about this noise. In fact, the whole scene was bizarre in the extreme, with men and women gathered in groups, drinking some obviously strong beverages, smoking, and watching the grotesque antics of the young women. It reminded Mathias of something he had read concerning the strange antics of ancient uncivilized aboriginal tribes on various continents of Earth, yet he knew that these Earthlings were supposedly civilized.

Watching the confusing scene before him, Mathias became aware of a group of men who were standing on the platform with the two sparsely dressed young women. The men seemed to be grabbing, or attempting to grab, the two women. Each time they did, though, their hands passed through the women with no effect. As they failed in their attempts to touch the girls, Mathias could hear and feel the agony and frustration of their faltering efforts. Startled, Mathias was suddenly aware that these men were spirits, with no auras, who were attempting some type of action with the girls. He asked: *Who are they, and what're they doing?*

These are spirits, said Brother Parley, *who've completed their Earthly lives. They spent most of their time on Earth responding to Satan's prompting. What you see are these individuals attempting to satisfy their sexual appetites and being extremely frustrated because they've lost all ability in this regard. They are stuck on Earth in their own private hell. You'll observe that they can't see us, nor are they aware of other spirits who are trying to help them. They're trapped by the impure thoughts and habits they developed during Earth-life.*

Mathias looked around the room and was surprised to see other brightly glowing spirits. He could feel their spirits and the greeting that they communicated to him. He saw that they were hovering over several in the room, but no one seemed to notice them. Many in the room were, obviously, Earthlings, who seemed to be enjoying the noise and confusion. Surrounding these Earthlings were numerous disembodied spirits with no auras. The Earthlings appeared totally oblivious to the spirits near them, and both groups did not recognize the few glowing spirits in the room.

Glancing at a group surrounding a corner table, Mathias became fascinated by their actions. They were drinking from bottles of the strong beverages, and they seemed very amused about something they were doing. One young woman, dressed in a short-tight black dress, had a piece of paper upon which she poured a vial of white powder. Encouraged by two men at the table, she sniffed the powder up her nose, and they all laughed uproariously. Also watching, and very close to the woman, were three or four spirits who seemed anxious about something. The Earthlings at the table could be distinguished from the watching spirits by the fact that each Earthling had a small aura—not the brilliant aura and glowing light of Brother Parley and his companions, but an aura nevertheless.

As Mathias watched in horror, the woman dressed in black slouched over the table—apparently in some type of unconscious stupor—accompanied by much laughter by her companions. With incredulity, Mathias saw the woman slump over; then the small aura that surrounded her seemed to part, and instantly one of the female spirits that had been anxiously watching the antics of those at the table seemed to jump into the slumped form. Where there had been two individuals previously, now there was one. Laura had witnessed the scene also, and Mathias could feel of her abhorrence to what she had seen.

Sensing the disgust of his companions, and sharing some of that feeling, but also feeling pity and love for the pitiful beings in front of them, Brother Parley transmitted: *You've witnessed one of the tragedies of Earth. Satan and his followers have so influenced these poor disembodied spirits that they no longer are able to make free choices—these spirits are prisoners of their own unhealthy passions and habits.*

Brother Parley continued: *You probably observed the parting of the Earthling woman's protective aura. When the spirit and physical body are in a healthy condition, a protective aura—an energy field from the spirit—surrounds it. As this poor woman became unconscious from the effects of the various drugs she'd taken, her aura was weakened and the waiting disembodied spirit was able to take advantage of her condition and enter her body. These unfortunate spirits are so obsessed with the desire to again feel the sensations that they've become prisoner to that they'll do almost anything to gain access to another body—even one that's unconscious.*

Emotional distress from fear, hate, anger, greed, and lust can create the same vulnerable condition in the spirit that you just witnessed. On the other hand, healthy emotions, such as love, charity, sympathy, and mercy can protect the spirit from the evil intrusions of Satan and his followers. Above all, prayer to the Father and the Son renders Earthlings relatively immune from the advances of Satan.

You've seen what I wanted to show you from this place. Let's now travel to another of Satan's domains.

Accelerating from the unpleasant atmosphere they had just been in, Mathias was relieved to leave the place. Wondering what they would meet next, he stayed close to Brother Parley and Laura. They traveled briefly over Earth when suddenly they were enveloped by complete darkness. It was blackness such as Mathias had never encountered. He could not even see the glowing forms of Parley and Laura. Fortunately, he could feel their presence, and Brother Parley transmitted: *Stay close, both of you.*

As they traveled in this complete blackness, Mathias became aware of other presences near them. He seemed to have stopped moving, and there was a sense of agony and distress surrounding him. Mathias reached into the darkness with his hand, and he immediately withdrew it upon being greeted by an unholy screech. The sound was a cross between an angry growl and a cry of pain. Mathias could feel the presence of a being in extreme agony.

Moving closer to Brother Parley and Laura, the welcome thought transmission of Brother Parley calmed him. *What you're feeling is the torment of many spirits who failed during their life's sojourn on Earth. The cry of pain you heard and felt was from an individual who was killed in a shoot-out with a policeman. His entire life was wasted in the fruitless pursuit of his greedy passions. Now he must pass, what to him, is an eternity of time in this complete blackness.*

Is he aware of our presence? Laura asked.

No, Brother Parley answered. *He's only aware of his own misery. He's not even conscious of the other miserable spirits around him. They're all driven by contempt for themselves and for what they did with their lives.*

Could other superior beings help them from their personal dungeons? Mathias asked.

Not in their present spiritual state, continued Brother Parley. *They'd be even more miserable to be in the presence of Superior Beings, much less in the presence of the Father and the Son. This extended period in their private hells is necessary preparation. Most of them, if given a choice, would extinguish themselves as conscious beings.*

Let's leave, pled Mathias. Laura smiled as she received his thought, and Brother Parley transmitted: *All right, but I'm not sure you'll like the next place any better.*

Sensing motion, Mathias moved closer to his two companions. He enjoyed the sensation of the nearness of Laura, but even she was not able to mitigate against the despair he'd felt in the total darkness. As they moved on, Mathias was able to see light ahead. Unfortunately, the feeling of dread within him persisted.

Initially, the group emerged into what seemed a large hole with beings clinging to the sides of the hole. What light there was had a reddish cast, and the spirit beings, as with the previous beings, seemed racked with anguish. Mathias felt the distress of the clinging spirits as his group descended further into the hole.

The reddish light became brighter, accompanied by a feeling of intense heat, when suddenly the hole opened to an immense cavern covered by a lake of burning material. Within the lake were islands of smoldering rock, and perched on the rocks were other spirit beings in obvious agony. Their cries of pain and misery stabbed at Mathias until his own pain seemed to match theirs.

Some of the spirits appeared in form to be only partly human, with strangely grotesque heads and bodies. Many were attacking other beings around them, but with no success since they were unable to grip each other. There was a filthy stench which permeated the atmosphere, and the stinking atmosphere echoed with the moans, wails, and cries from the damned creatures below. The scene was truly a view of the abyss of hell.

Feeling as if he were about to become one of the damned creatures he was viewing, Mathias orally screamed: "Get us out of here."

Emerging from the cavern, or whatever it was, into a brilliant star-lit night, Mathias embraced his two companions in order to feel again of their love, and thus to recover his equanimity. They were standing on the top of a large mesa in the midst of a desert, and the stars seemed to twinkle in gentle reassurance that all would be well. Reveling in the peace and silence of the night, no one interrupted the reverie for some time. Finally, Mathias said: "Thank you for getting us out of that. I couldn't have taken any more of what I saw and felt. Who were those poor spirits, and where were they?"

Brother Parley responded: "As The Word says: 'These are they who are liars, and sorcerers, and adulterers, and whore-mongers, and whosoever loves and makes a lie. These are they who suffer the vengeance of eternal fire. These are they who are cast down to hell and suffer the wrath of Almighty God, until the fulness of times, when Christ shall have subdued all enemies under his feet, and shall have perfected his work.'

"As you witnessed," continued Brother Parley, "those unfortunate spirits are trapped in the horror of hell. It's a hell of their own making, and one from which they cannot escape."

"It's not a hell that continues forever, though, is it Brother Parley?" asked Laura.

"To the poor spirits suffering through it, it'll seem forever. But, as The Word I just quoted said, it'll end in the fullness of times when the Son has completed his work. The Word, elsewhere says: 'Behold, I am endless, and the punishment which is given from my hand is endless punishment, for Endless is my name. Wherefore—Eternal punishment is God's punishment.' Thus, Endless Punishment is the Lord's punishment, and even that punishment terminates at the final judgment when the Son has subdued all enemies of The Word."

"So what will happen to them, then?" asked Mathias.

"They'll be judged with all of Father's children, they'll receive an indestructible physical body, and they'll be assigned a glory commensurate with how they lived on Earth—probably the Telestial, or lowest, Kingdom. Even though they'll be released from hell at that time, their damnation will continue in the sense that they'll be unable to realize the full potential that they could have. The Word, as written by the prophet Abinadi in The Book of Mormon, puts it this way:

> Even this mortal shall put on immortality, and this corruption shall put on incorruption, and shall be brought to stand before the bar of God, to be judged of him according to their works whether they be good or whether they be evil—
>
> If they be good, to the resurrection of endless life and happiness; and if they be evil, to the resurrection of endless damnation, being delivered up to the devil, who hath subjected them, which is damnation—
>
> Having gone according to their own carnal wills and desires; having never called upon the Lord while the arms of mercy were extended towards them; for the arms of mercy were extended towards them, and they would not; they being warned of their iniquities and yet they would not depart from them; and they were commanded to repent and yet they would not repent.
>
> And now, ought ye not to tremble and repent of your sins, and remember that only in and through Christ ye can be saved?

"After the judgment and resurrection of these poor souls, then their pain will be the knowledge that they'll *never* reach the potential or the glory that they might have. Still, the glory of the Telestial will be beyond anything those in the spirit prison could hope for based on their adherence to the Lord's law. Due to the atonement of the Son, though, and through his mercy, they'll live in a measure of glory. The prophet, Joseph Smith, said this about the release of the spirit prisoners from hell:

> Let your hearts rejoice, and be exceedingly glad. Let the earth break forth into singing. Let the dead speak forth anthems of eternal praise to the King Immanuel, who hath ordained, before the world was, that which would enable us to

redeem them out of their prison; for the prisoners shall go free.

So, you see, even these unfortunates will live in an eternal bliss suitable to their spiritual development."

Laura interrupted Brother Parley's thought by asking: "Where'll you take us next, Brother Parley? Are you going to show us more about Satan's work?"

"Perhaps a little more. But I'll also show you of the Son's work on Earth. For the moment, though, let's savor the remainder of Earth's night by enjoying our Quiet. And let's offer prayers of gratitude for The Plan which allows each of us the freedom of choice to grow to our ultimate potential."

Mathias entered his Quiet, separate from Laura, on a beautiful flattened mountain top that seemed to have been placed in the middle of a spectacular desert area—at least by Earth's standards it was spectacular. Expressing gratitude in his prayer for his many blessings, he was amazed that he actually felt refreshed by what he had been through. Having seen the worst consequences of disobeying The Word, and still understanding how everything fit within The Plan, gave him great confidence.

Earth was fearsome, just as Mathias thought, but it was not randomly so. Everything had an impact on everything else, and it all contributed to the magnificence of The Plan. If his knowledge of Earth continued to advance as rapidly as it had in his recent experiences, he should be able to commit to a life on Earth.

Chapter 8

ANCESTORS IN WAITING

Behold, I will send you Elijah the prophet before the coming of the great and dreadful day of the Lord:
And he shall turn the heart of the fathers to the children, and the heart of the children to their fathers, lest I come and smite the earth with a curse. [1]

The Sun-Star was just rising above the horizon, and Mathias had completed his Quiet on the Mancos Mesa of southern Utah. Although the view from the Mesa was not as glorious as that from Mount Isaiah on Kolob-1, with its view of the Valley of the Son, Mathias had to admit that Earth also had spectacular beauty. His Quiet, with its prayers and meditation, had further calmed his spirit, and Mathias felt that he was ready for whatever Brother Parley had to offer.

Receiving a thought-signal from Brother Parley, Mathias wished himself to the area of the Mesa where Brother Parley was. Laura was already there, and she smiled her love and embraced him.

"What've you got for us on this Earth-day, Brother Parley? I'm ready for anything," Mathias said enthusiastically.

Brother Parley smiled, and said, "That's a wonderful attitude, Mathias, especially after your experiences in Satan's realm. This Earth-day will be equally interesting, but in a different way.

---

1 *The Holy Bible*, Malachi 4:5-6.

83

Today you'll see some of what the Son has done to offset the influence of Satan. But first . . . yes, he's almost here."

"Who's almost here, Brother Parley?" asked Laura.

"Your guide for this Earth-day. His Earth-name was Olvin Blair, and you'll know him as Brother Olvin."

"But why do we need another guide? Aren't you going to be with us?" Laura asked.

"No. My duties on Kolob-1 are pressing, and I must get back. You'll find that Brother Olvin is just right for your special needs. Ah, . . . here he is now."

Suddenly, as Brother Parley finished speaking, another glowing spirit appeared. From the brightness of his form and robe, and his aura, Mathias understood that he was a superior being with priesthood power. Love infused the group as each spirit bathed in the glory of the newly arrived spirit. Feelings of déjà vu filled Mathias, and he was not sure why. *Could he have known Brother Olvin from some previous time? Or, was Brother Olvin to be important in his future? Or, . . . what was it?*

Still musing about Brother Olvin, who smiled at Mathias and expressed his love, Mathias looked at Brother Parley in time to see the light gather about him as he disappeared. Then Brother Olvin began speaking orally.

"You were promised yester-Earth-day, by Brother Parley, that on this Earth-day you'd see more of Satan's work, and you'd also see some of the Son's work to offset Satan. For these purposes we'll first travel to the New Brunswick, Canada, area of North America. That's the area where I spent most of my birth-life. Let's travel swiftly. I know that you enjoy traveling slowly over Earth so that you can observe the different features and the beauty of Earth, but we've little Earth-time to accomplish what we should, so stay close to me."

Passing over the continent, the blur of sky and clouds was so rapid that Mathias had little consciousness of the trip. The first view that he was aware of was of a seascape with a coastal region, rolling hills beyond the coast, and a city at the mouth of a large river. The river emptied into a large bay, and on the opposite side of the bay from the large city was a smaller city—white ships seemed to be traveling between the two cities.

Brother Olvin transmitted the thought: *The large city is St. John, the largest city, and a seaport, of the Province of New Brunswick. Travel back and forth between St. John, and Digby, on the Province of Nova Scotia, is made possible by the ferry boats you see traveling between the two areas. I lived inland from the city of St. John, near the city of Fredericton, which is upriver from St. John. As we descend on St. John, I want you to keep your spiritual senses alert and you'll see a city above a city.*

Mathias was not sure what Brother Olvin meant by a "city above a city," but after what he had been through with Brother Parley he was ready for anything. Looking around as they descended, suddenly Mathias was aware of a park-like area with trees, flowers, lawns and paths. The city of St. John had disappeared, and this area seemed to be superimposed above it.

Sensing the confusion in both Laura and Mathias, Brother Olvin transmitted: *So you see it, do you? That's good—it means that your spiritual senses are being developed properly. Earthlings, the residents of St. John, are not aware of this spiritual city above their city. We shall spend some time here, so watch carefully what happens.*

Receiving a thought transmission from Laura, Mathias looked toward her and was surprised as she directed his gaze to large groups of people coming from a forest area ahead of them. There was some type of game that the people were engaged in, and they were talking and laughing as they progressed. The game apparently consisted of hitting a ball with a mallet through hoops placed in the lawn. The people were all dressed in clothes that seemed strangely out-of-place from those that he had seen other Earthlings wear. Mathias had the impression that they were from an earlier age.

Being curious about the activities he was witnessing, Mathias asked: *What are they doing, and who are they?*

Just watch, said Brother Olvin, *and concentrate on the people.*

Following Brother Olvin's instruction, Mathias watched a group of people that were hitting their ball toward Mathias and his companions. The people seemed totally oblivious to the presence of Mathias, Laura and Brother Olvin.

Suddenly Mathias was astonished to find that he understood who the people were—at least, in part. He excitedly transmitted: *Look, Laura, that man in front is the husband of the lady next to him, and the other three people are their children. The lady, in the large hoop-like dress, is the sister of the wife. And the people in the group following—they're all related to each other.*

Laura was puzzled and transmitted: *How did you know that, Mathias? Are they really related?* she asked Brother Olvin.

Yes, they're all related, just as Mathias said. Actually, they are ancestors of mine through the Blair line. They've completed their time on Earth and are gathered here until they can be released.

What do you mean, released, Brother Olvin? Are these people held captive, or something? asked Laura.

Yes, they're held captive by their own habits and thoughts. As The Word says:

> *Behold, these are they who died without the law; . . .*

> *Who received not the testimony of Jesus in the flesh, but afterwards received it.*

> *These are they who are honorable men of the earth, who were blinded by the craftiness of men.*

I understand, now, Brother Olvin. These spirits are from people who weren't terribly bad, as the others were whom we saw with Brother Parley. But they're still prisoners until they accept The Word. Can they be taught, or are they trapped until the resurrection, as most of those we saw yester-Earth-day were?

You understand correctly, Laura. And, yes, some of them can be taught. The Word also says:

> *But behold, from among the righteous, he organized his forces and appointed messengers, clothed with power and authority, and commissioned them to go forth and carry the light of the gospel to them that were in darkness, even to all the spirits of men; and thus was the gospel preached to the dead.*

Look, for example, at that other group near the little stream, and tell me what you see.

Looking in the direction suggested by Brother Olvin, Mathias observed several people, whose relationship he seemed to know, in a classroom-type situation. An individual in front of them, dressed in white, and with a glowing aura, seemed to be teaching the others. Alongside of the male spirit was a female clothed in white and with a brilliant aura. Mathias understood that she was the wife of the male teacher.

Mathias transmitted: *That superior being, the one in white, appears to be a Priesthood-power spirit, and he's related to the others whom he's teaching. Is that correct?*

That's right, Mathias; as you suggest, he's related, and he has the Priesthood authority of the Son. His eternal companion is helping. They're teaching the other spirits The Word, and as you can see, the others are listening.

I still don't understand why so many spirits are playing those strange games, commented Laura. *Look down there in the large field. There must be thousands of people, either involved in the game where they kick the ball, or as spectators. Why are they wasting their time?*

The game is called soccer, and they're doing what interested them on Earth. It wasn't an evil activity when they were passing through their birth-life, but, as you can see, it doesn't contribute to their progression in this life. On Earth the game was useful in teaching lessons of cooperation, team-work, and how to overcome obstacles, but as with many other Earthly pursuits, if allowed to become an obsession, it can be bad. Many of the people you see playing the game have become obsessed with the importance of the game rather than seeing it as another teaching experience. That's why it's so important that they be taught—in a similar manner to the smaller group by the stream.

If teaching them is so important, why aren't there more teachers helping with the other groups? asked Laura.

Because there aren't enough of us in their family tree who've learned and accepted The Word. I have two sons on Earth who, with their families, have embraced The Word, but that doesn't help me over here. I have a third son, Johnny, who's rejected The Word. Because of the limited number of those who have knowledge of The Word and can teach it, the other spirits who might receive it will just have to wait until we can get to them. If the need is urgent, then we can occasionally take other steps.

How urgent is urgent? thought transmitted Mathias, and they all chuckled.

Let me show you, transmitted Brother Olvin. Directing Laura and Mathias to follow him, they traveled a short distance to the base of a large tree. Standing under the tree was an attractive man who was watching most of the other spirits as they played their games. As Mathias, Laura and Brother Olvin approached the man, he looked at each of them. It was apparent that, unlike the other spirits in the area, this individual could see them. He was totally conscious of their presence.

Gasping in astonishment, Laura transmitted: *My word, that man is . . . and he knows me.* Filled with revulsion, she desperately wanted to leave his presence.

Who is he? asked Mathias.

Tell Mathias who he is, Laura, communicated Brother Olvin.

He is . . . Laura was filled with repugnance, and she was unable to continue.

He was known as The Son of the Morning at one time, transmitted Brother Olvin. *Now he's known as Satan, and yes, Laura, he knows you intimately.*

What's he doing here? asked Mathias.

He's attempting to influence those spirits in my family line so that they won't listen to me or to others of us who're trying to bring them The Word. There are many helpers of Satan, also. Their objective is to make others miserable as they themselves are and to prevent the progress of those we are working with.

Looking around, for the first time Mathias noticed a group of spirits with no auras. Most of those playing games had weak auras, but the particular spirits he was looking at did not. They seemed to be encouraging the others in their games.

May we leave this area, Brother Olvin? Laura asked.

Of course, Laura. We've accomplished what we came to do.
With that thought from Brother Olvin, Laura and Mathias found
themselves standing, with Brother Olvin, on a gently rising hill
overlooking the ocean. It was a beautiful, and a refreshing view
that calmed their troubled spirits.

*There's one thing that still troubles me, Brother Olvin. I don't
understand . . .*

"Let's speak orally, now. It's less efficient, I know, but it's
more in line with what you'll do on Earth. What is it that you
don't understand, Laura?"

"How is it that Mathias knew the relationships of the spirits
that we saw, and I didn't?"

Brother Olvin smiled. "Let's see if Mathias has guessed why
he knew them. What do you think about her question, Mathias?"

"Could it be . . . that is, am I to be born into the Blair line?"

"Yes, Mathias. If you accept the calling that the Brethren will
give you, you'll be born into my line. In fact, you'll be my
grandson. As I mentioned earlier, I have three sons, two of whom
are vigorously involved in promulgating The Word. One of my
sons, Jim Blair, lives in Price, Utah, with his wife Lori and their
children. Jim and Lori are good friends with Janis and Alma Pratt
into whose line Laura will be born.

"Jim and Lori are about to have their fourth child, and you
won't be born to them. My other son, Alvin and his wife, Sue,
live in San Jose, California. They'd like another child, their third,
and you'll be born into their family—if you accept."

"Oh, Mathias," Laura squealed, "that's how we'll get
together. The Blairs and the Pratts in Utah are good friends, and
it will be through them that we'll meet."

Brother Olvin smiled. "It could work out that way, Laura, but
let's see what Mathias thinks. What about it, Mathias?"

Gathering his emotions, Mathias struggled. He loved Laura
so, and he didn't want to hurt her. But he still wasn't ready to
make a complete commitment to Earth—with all of its difficulties.
What he had seen in the last two Earth-days was enough to frighten
the bravest of spirits. His understanding of The Plan had been
strengthened immensely, but he needed to know more about how

the Spirit could help good, but confused, mortals struggling through Earth life's pitfalls. Being certain that he would need such help if he chose Earth, he needed a little more information.

Choosing his words carefully, Mathias began: "It would be wonderful if Laura and I could get together on Earth, and if I can . . . I love her dearly. Could I have some more time to think and pray about it, though? I'm not sure that I . . ."

"Of course you may have some more time, Mathias. The call, when it comes, will be from Brother Brigham. In the meantime, use your Quiets to good advantage. If you do, you'll make the proper decision when the time comes.

"Now there's one last thing that I want you to see before we return to Kolob-1. Earlier, I promised you that I'd show you something of the Son's work to offset Satan's efforts. There are many magnificent accomplishments by good people working on behalf of the Son, but this effort, in particular, I want you to see. We'll travel to the small city of Manti, Utah, for that purpose.

Reducing altitude and speed, the three spirits came into view of Manti. Sitting high on a hill with carefully manicured lawns was a white building with two rounded towers. In the gardens surrounding the building was a small group of people talking in animated tones. Brother Olvin led Laura and Mathias to the group, and they listened. A young woman was speaking.

"We really appreciate your helping today, Janis and Alma, and you too, Jeremy. We had these names processed on 'Temple Ready,' and I'm not sure how much longer I have before I have to deliver my baby, so we needed to get the work done. I know how busy you are with work, Alma, and with your duties as bishop, so I know it's a real sacrifice."

"It's no sacrifice, Lori, to do the Lord's work in his temple. There's nothing that Jeremy would rather do than be with Jeff. Isn't that true Jeremy?"

Jeremy looked embarrassed and said: "Yes."

"When is your due-date, Lori?" asked the first young woman.

"The doctor says the baby should arrive in the next two weeks. Jim says that I can have two days off from cooking meals."

They laughed, and her husband changed the subject with: "Let's hope it's not today. . . . If we're going to meet your 9:00 a.m. baptismal date, though, we'd better go inside and change."

Following the family groups inside the temple, Laura, Mathias and Brother Olvin observed as they changed into white clothes and then went to the baptismal font. They watched as one of the men went into the water and then held out his hand for the oldest boy to enter. Instructing the boy how to stand next to him, he then raised his arm to the square and pronounced the words: "Jeffery Pratt, you acting as proxy for Thornton Blair, who is dead; Having been commissioned of Jesus Christ, I baptize you in the name of the Father, and of the Son, and of the Holy Ghost. Amen." The boy was then immersed in the water, after which he emerged with a smile on his face.

Repeating this process several times, the young man changed places with the other man, and a girl entered the water with him. She was baptized for several deceased women. During the baptisms, the three spirits watched reverently by the side. Then Brother Olvin transmitted the thought: *Look over near the far wall and tell me what you see.*

Mathias looked at the far wall and noticed a number of spirits, with bright auras, standing up near the ceiling. He immediately understood their relationship to each other—they were all related, either through marriage or directly, to the Blair line. As he watched the spirits react to their baptisms, he felt of their great love for those performing the work, and he understood the feelings they transmitted of relief and rapture.

I see spirits watching as their baptisms are performed, Laura transmitted, *and I can feel of their love and gratitude. Are they all related to you, Brother Olvin?*

Yes Laura, they are all my ancestors, either directly through the Blair line, or through marriage. It's a wonderful day for them, for now their progression is assured. I share with them the feelings of joy that they have.

Continuing with his thought transmission, Brother Olvin communicated: *The selfless work performed by thousands of dedicated Earthlings working in the Son's temples throughout the world can only be measured in the record books of heaven—and measured it will be. Satan may attempt to slow or stop the work, but he'll fail. Angels will sing ecstatically the praise of those performing this labor of love.*

Now, we've done all that we came to do, so let's return home—home to Kolob-1.

Chapter 9

A DEATH AND A BIRTH

There is no cause to fear death; it is but an incident in life. It is as natural as birth. Why should we fear it? Some fear it because they think it is the end of life, and life often is the dearest thing we have. Eternal life is man's greatest blessing. [1]

Driving to work at the Hunter Plant, Alma and Jim were, as usual, talking about a problem at work. They both seemed under some stress, and Jim was talking.

"Roger Talbot, from Engineering, and I are driving to Naughton to see how they're doing fixing that part for our turbine. We'll call you from there and let you know what we find."

"That's a good idea, Jim. Why don't you charter Sunwest Aviation, though? It'd be quicker."

"They're predicting a major winter storm in the Wyoming area, and Sunwest doesn't like to fly into the Kemmerer airport when the weather's bad. We'll be okay; we're taking one of the four-wheel drive vehicles. And we have a radio."

"Drive carefully. We don't want an accident when your baby is due. What about the baby? When is it scheduled to arrive?"

---

1 McKay, David O., 1873-1970, *Conference Report*, April 1966, p. 58, published by The Church of Jesus Christ of Latter-day Saints, Salt Lake City, Utah.

"Lori has promised me faithfully that she won't have the baby before I get back," Jim laughed. "Actually, the doctor said that it'll be a week yet, anyhow."

"Well, be careful on your trip."

"I will, Alma. By the way, Lori and I really appreciated your helping with the temple work the other day. She wanted to get the work done before the baby came. You helped us greatly."

"It was our pleasure. Janis is into genealogy about as much as Lori is. I wish I could get as excited about it as she does."

"I know what you mean. Lori is almost fanatic on the issue, and the funny thing is that she's working mostly on my line. She claims that she feels an urgency about the Blair genealogy. Don't ask me why. There certainly is no urgency from my point of view," Jim laughed. "After the session the other day, Lori said she was certain that some of my ancestors were present during the performance of the ordinances. I didn't feel anything, though, did you?"

"No, but I was hungry. Maybe I was thinking about my stomach." They both laughed. "Women must be more spiritually attuned than men," Alma commented.

"I think you're right. Wasn't it Janis who got the feeling that you should have another child?"

"Yes, and it was more than a feeling. I'll tell you about it sometime."

"Is Janis pregnant yet?"

"No, but I'm doing my best," Alma laughed.

"I'm sure it'll happen in time, otherwise Janis wouldn't have had her experience."

"No doubt that's true, Jim. Well, here we are. Have a good trip to the big town of Kemmerer. And do drive carefully."

❦   ❦   ❦   ❦

Meeting with the warehouse people to review the status of the latest inventory, Alma was looking forward to quitting time. It had been a busy day, and he was tired. Unfortunately, Jim had scheduled him for a full range of interviews in his bishop's office tonight, so he'd only have time for a quick dinner. He knew that he'd feel refreshed once he started interviewing the young people, though. They were great kids.

Nancy, Alma's secretary, stood by the door of the conference room and looked distressed. "What is it, Nancy?" he asked.

"There's a Highway Patrol officer here, Sergeant Jensen, and he says that it's important he meet with you."

Alma was mildly annoyed. Just as he was trying to get ready to close the work-day. It wasn't uncommon for people to seek him out with different problems, but he wondered what the Highway Patrol wanted with him. Maybe one of his people had too many tickets.

"Show him to my office. I'll be there shortly."

Entering his office a few minutes later, Alma offered his hand to the Highway Patrol officer, who rose on his entry. The patrolman seemed nervous, and Alma tried to put him at ease by smiling as they shook hands. "What can we do for you, Sergeant?

Sergeant Jensen remained serious—his hand had been sweaty when Alma shook it, and he continued to exhibit nervousness.

"What is it, Sergeant?"

"Do you have two employees by the names of Roger Talbot and Jim Blair?"

Feeling a stab of anxiety and dread, Alma responded, "Yes, I do. Why?"

"Wyoming Highway Patrol just called us and informed us of a bad accident fifteen miles south of Kemmerer. Apparently there was a white-out in the current storm, and the highway was icy. Anyway, the vehicle driven by your employees lost control and flipped several times. One of your employees is injured and is in the local hospital in Kemmerer—it doesn't appear that his injuries are life threatening. The driver of the vehicle, though, was killed."

Swallowing hard to control his emotions, Alma asked: "Do you know which employee was killed?"

"According to Wyoming Patrol, the driver was Jim Blair. He was the one who was killed."

Struggling to control the black feeling of despair and hopelessness that engulfed him, Alma could not speak for a moment or two. He watched the patrolman who also seemed to be having difficulty continuing. Finally, with difficulty, Sergeant Jensen asked: "Do you have information on next of kin? And do you want to notify them, or should we?"

"We have the information, Sergeant. We'll take care of it, and thank you."

Collapsing into his chair and staring out the window, Alma tried to focus on the enormity of what he had just been told. His mind did not want to work, yet he knew that quick action was called for. He felt a momentary despair that was almost overwhelming. Forcing himself to address the needed issues, he buzzed his secretary.

❦   ❦   ❦   ❦

Arriving at the Blair home with Thelma Hoffman, the ward Relief Society President, Alma was relieved to see the three children playing in the front yard. "Hi, Jeff," said Alma. "Is your mother home?"

"Yeah, she's in the kitchen, Bishop. Should I get her?"

"We'll just ring the doorbell, Jeff. Thanks anyway."

Lori came to the door, looking very pregnant, with her hands covered with flour. She smiled when she saw them and said: "Why, Bishop, and Thelma. How nice to see you. Come in. I was just making some cookies for my tribe."

Seeing the serious expressions on the faces of Alma and Thelma, Lori grew uneasy. In fact, she had been uneasy all day—since the previous evening when she had experienced a premonition that something horrible was about to happen.

Steeling herself for what must be coming, Lori said, as calmly as she could: "Do sit. You seem so serious. Is something the matter?"

"Well, yes. It's just that we have to . . ." Alma was silent for a moment as he grappled with his own emotions.

With rising fear, and with a shaky voice, Lori asked, "It's Jim, isn't it?"

"Yes, Lori, it's Jim."

"I knew it. I felt it last night. Is he . . . is he dead?"

"He was . . . he was killed in a car crash near Kemmerer about three o'clock this afternoon. The Highway Patrol just notified us."

Lori sat in a chair and began to cry softly. She put her arms around her stomach as if to protect her unborn child. The awful reality of the loss of Jim, her beloved, her marvelously strong husband, engulfed her. How would she . . . how could she continue without him? And what about the new baby—and the other children?

Thelma sat beside her and embraced her. After a moment, Lori said: "I'll be all right. Even though I knew, it was . . ." A couple of sobs shook Lori's body. "The final realization of what happened is still painful, isn't it?"

Summoning all of his resolve, Alma spoke as calmly as he could: "Yes, Lori, it is. We'll do all we can, though, to soften the blow."

"I understand, Bishop. Thank you for coming. . . . I know it was hard, and . . ."

Lori's body shook with more sobs as she thought of her children. How could she tell them that their father would no longer be here? Her devastating emotions would aggravate the situation and make it worse for the children. They had to be told, but she couldn't . . . Maybe . . .

Between sobs, Lori choked out, "Bishop, could you . . . would you help me with the children? They must be told."

Suppressing a surge of fear, Alma asked, "Would you like me to tell them now?"

"Could you, please, Bishop? They respect you so much, and I . . . I don't think I could get through it."

"Call them in, Lori."

Moving with difficulty to the door, Lori called Jeff, who was twelve, Alice, who was nine, and Ruth, who was seven. They came running into the house, and they seated themselves on the sofa where Lori joined them. She managed to say: "Children, the Bishop has something to tell you."

Saying a silent prayer, Alma commenced what was, for him, the most difficult speech he had ever given. Keeping his emotions under check with extreme difficulty, he said: "Children, there's been a very bad accident, and Heavenly Father has . . . He's called your father home to heaven. Your father won't be here physically any more to help you, but he'll visit you spiritually. You'll each have to be brave and help your mother."

The children looked at their mother, who was wiping her eyes with a handkerchief, and their eyes got wide. Jeff asked with a faltering voice: "Do you mean, Bishop, that Dad has . . . that Dad has been killed?"

Temporarily unable to subdue his own grief, tears streamed from Alma's eyes. After wiping them and taking a couple of deep breaths, he managed to say: "Yes, Jeff, that's what I mean. Do you think you can help your mother—especially when the new baby comes?"

"I'll help her, Bishop," Jeff said with his lower lip quivering.

Alice and Ruth ran into their mother's arms, sobbing. Putting her arms around them, Lori joined them in crying. After a time, when the sobs had subsided somewhat, Alma said: "Lori, I'll leave you with Thelma for a while. I need to meet with Bishop Jarvis of the Eighth Ward so that we can call on Julie Talbot and tell her about Roger. He was injured in the same accident with Jim. He's in the Kemmerer hospital, and we need to get Julie up there with him."

"That's okay, Bishop, you do what you need to. Thelma will help me."

"I'll be back later this evening, Lori. You probably already know that Jim was completely covered with company insurance. The insurance people will be here tomorrow morning and tell you exactly where you stand. I assure you that you'll have no immediate financial worries."

"Thank you, Bishop."

"You're welcome, Lori. Tomorrow afternoon, when you've had a chance to sort out your thoughts, I'll be by to help you plan the funeral. Our people will see that Jim is brought down from Kemmerer to a local mortuary. Please know that everything will be all right."

"I know it will, Bishop. Could you . . . that is, could you come later in the evening and give the children and me a blessing?"

"Of course I will, Lori. And God bless you."

❦   ❦   ❦   ❦

Lori was not sure how she got through the funeral, but she did—in fact it seemed to help both her and the children. The Bishop was superb, and what he said about Jim was just right. The Relief Society made everything easier with the guests from out-of-state. She was glad that Mother Blair stayed with her and the children. They loved their grandmother, and her presence seemed to calm them. She offered, and Lori agreed, for her to stay and help with the new baby's arrival.

The Bishop's blessing was what helped the most, though. Among other blessings, the Bishop promised her that the baby would not arrive until after the funeral, and that she and the baby would be protected during this period. Being assured in the blessing that she would have the strength to do what she needed for herself and the children gave her great peace of mind. Ever since the blessing, Lori had the feeling that, despite the catastrophe of Jim's loss, everything would be okay.

Jim's brother, Alvin, and his wife, Sue, from San Jose, California, were marvelous. They stayed with one of the other ward families, and they fit right in with the members of the ward. She knew that getting through the eulogy was difficult for Alvin, but his touch of humor from their youth, mixed with his knowledge of eternal life, was most appreciated. Even the children seemed to understand the great bond that existed between Jim and Alvin.

Many of the workers from Utah Power attended the funeral. Holding the funeral in the stake center, as the Bishop suggested, was fortunate in view of the large crowd from the company. The flowers that the company provided were absolutely beautiful, and several of Jim's friends from work served as pall bearers.

Thinking back on the funeral, and how it helped her to get through the crisis of losing Jim, Lori felt peace within herself. She was now ready for the birth of her child. If only. . . . Aside from the terrible loss of Jim, there was only one troubling aspect that still bothered her. It was Jim's brother, Johnny, . . . or Professor John Blair as he preferred to be known.

Having lived all her life in the Price region, Lori had never been close to Johnny or his wife Barbara. Teaching at the University of California in Berkeley as a full professor of philosophy, and his wife being a professor of law at the same institution, made it difficult for Lori and Jim to relate to them. Jim tried, Lori knew, and when Johnny got his doctorate at Harvard University, Jim and his parents traveled there to witness the ceremony. It was a disappointment, though, because Johnny had social commitments that prevented him from spending more than an hour or two with Jim and his parents. Johnny and Barbara had no children, and Lori wondered if they had decided against children because of their professional commitments.

Knowing that Mother Blair, and Father Blair when he was alive, were hurt when Johnny asked for his name to be removed from the records of the church, she understood some of the tension between the families. She was unaware, however, of the significant tension that existed between Alvin and Johnny. She had hoped that when Johnny agreed to come to the funeral it would be an occasion for renewed family love. Just the opposite had been true. Alvin and Johnny hardly spoke, and when they did speak it was usually Alvin responding to some caustic comment made by Johnny.

Alvin and Sue were returning to Salt Lake tomorrow to catch the plane to San Jose. Riding as far as Salt Lake with them would be Johnny, where he would catch his plane for Oakland. Lori hoped that they could travel that far in peace.

Driving in silence for a time, Alvin and Sue quietly reviewed in their minds the last few days with Lori. Johnny sat in the back with his own thoughts, mainly a feeling of distress that he could not smoke the cigarettes that he had in his coat pocket. If it had only been Alvin and he, Johnny would have smoked, just to irritate his brother, but out of consideration for Sue he reluctantly abstained.

"What do you think, Alvin, will she be okay?" Sue asked.

"Lori is a very strong lady, Sue. Jim left her with some wonderful children and with a tremendous heritage of faith. Her prayers—and ours—will help her. Yes, I think she'll be fine."

"You don't really believe that crap, do you Alvin?" intruded Johnny.

"What . . . what're you talking about, Johnny?"

"What you said about prayers—you don't really believe they offer any substantive help do you, other than as a mild psychological sedative?"

"Of course they help. Our Heavenly Father hears and answers prayers."

Laughing loudly, Johnny said: "Heavenly Father, my foot! Where was your Heavenly Father when Jim was killed? Why did he let a young man in the prime of life, with an expecting wife, and with three dependent children, get killed? I thought this mighty being was omniscient and able to help those in need. Where was Jim's help?—or maybe he didn't pray enough. What do you think?"

Responding angrily, Alvin said: "Of course Jim prayed. We talked about prayer often in the past, and of how prayers were answered. But I don't know why Heavenly Father allowed Jim to be killed. Maybe he was needed more on the other side than here."

Johnny laughed again. "I knew you'd say that. Religionists always use that cop-out when they try to explain the tragic death of someone. The fact is, there is no God, and there's no life after death. When you die, that's it, you're extinguished. The Bible is right in one sense, you came from dust, and you'll return to dust."

"The Bible also says that as in Adam all men die, so in Christ shall all be made alive."

"The Bible, little brother, is an allegoric collection of tales put there by superstitious clerics anxious to protect their position of power over the masses who couldn't read. Whenever a controversy arose about the most current view of God, a council was held to vote on whom and what God was. The Athanasian Creed, for example, spoke of: 'The Father Incomprehensible, the Son Incomprehensible, and the Holy Ghost Incomprehensible.' They're incomprehensible all right—unbelievable would be a better description."

"What about Joseph Smith and The Book of Mormon?"

"What about him?"

"How do you explain what he did?"

"Joseph Smith was an ignorant farm boy, with lots of charisma, who exercised his charm over his more ignorant followers."

"But The Book of Mormon . . ."

"Yes, The Book of Mormon! Joseph Smith, probably with the help of one of his more erudite followers, such as Oliver Cowdery, made up a story couched in a crude version of the King James English. Mark Twain was right when he characterized The Book of Mormon as chloroform in print."

"So you don't believe in God or in his son Jesus Christ?"

"Let me put it this way," and Johnny chuckled as he contemplated what he was about to say. "If they do exist they certainly are underachievers. For proof of that, all you have to do is look at the present state of the world."

"Do you believe in Satan?"

"Satan is a fictional character dreamed up by theologians to keep their religious flock in line. He's also useful as a frightening icon to squeeze more money out of the church adherents."

"Don't you think that religion has any value?"

"Oh, I suppose that it's a sort of emotional pit-stop for the weak, the troubled, and the superstitious."

"I know that you're smart, Johnny, but I feel sorry for you."

"Don't feel sorry for me, little brother. I'm getting mine out of this life, and I'm not constrained by some foolish 'thou shalt nots' written by a wild man who ate berries in the desert. Between what I make and my wife's salary, we make more money in a month than you'll make in a year of struggle, and I live in a view-home overlooking the San Francisco Bay. I publish in the most prestigious professional journals, and my colleagues acquiesce to my wisdom."

Knowing that he could not win an argument with his educated brother, and not knowing what to do, Alvin offered a short prayer so that he might know what to say. Upon completing his prayer he said: "I love you Johnny."

Being speechless for a moment, Johnny sputtered: "That's the frustrating thing about you, Alvin. What has love got to do with the conversation we were having? Whenever logic traps you, you respond with some non-sequitur."

"I love you Johnny."

Sitting upright in her hospital bed, Lori felt wonderful. The nurse had just brought her the new baby, and she was breast-feeding him. As he nuzzled and sucked, Lori was filled with such love and peace that she spilled some tears of gratitude onto his tiny head.

"Well, little one," she said, "how do you like this great big exciting world? You'll find that it's filled with love and opportunity, if you just look in the right places. Your Daddy understood that. What would you think if we named you after him? You couldn't have a better name—James Blair. Yes, that will be your name; we'll call you Jimmy. Welcome to the Blair family, Jimmy."

Chapter 10

A REUNION AND A CRISIS

I never saw a moor,
I never saw the sea;
Yet know I how the heather looks,
And what a wave must be.

I never spoke with God,
Nor visited in Heaven;
Yet certain am I of the spot
As if the chart were given. [1]

Since returning to Kolob-1, Mathias had been in teaching sessions with Brother Olvin. Through improved use of his Quiets he had been able to review a number of possible futures on Earth. These futures, in which he saw himself in a variety of circumstances, seemed realistic enough, but they always left him with a feeling of uncertainty. Explaining that they were only probable outcomes, and may or may not come true based upon how Mathias and others made their free choices, Brother Olvin told him not to put too much credence in what he saw in these futures. According to Brother Olvin, prayer, and Mathias's feelings from the Spirit were better measures of what might happen in the future.

Feeling better about Earth since he had learned so much more concerning it, Mathias was almost to the point that he could

---

1 Dickinson, Emily, 1830-1886, *I Never Saw a Moor*, 1865.

commit. He no longer had a desire to learn more about Krasak-3, but he still wondered if there were other bad things about Earth that he should know about.

Standing in a quiet glade in the Valley of the Son, Mathias was enjoying the quiet murmuring of a flowing brook. The sound from the brook was as though a happy chorus of children were frolicking in the glen. He wondered if Earth produced such ethereal sounds.

As he enjoyed his surroundings, Brother Olvin, whom Mathias had been waiting for, appeared. "I see that you got my thought transmission, Mathias. Thanks for waiting."

"I was enjoying the surroundings, Brother Olvin."

"This glade is lovely, and it was created for just such a purpose. I wanted to meet with you so that you could see two important events that're about to happen. One is certain, and one is not. They'll teach you much about Earth and how your activities there can affect your future."

"What kinds of events, Brother Olvin?"

"Both of them involve relatives of mine—and yours if you choose to join us—from Earth. My son, Jim, has just completed his fourth birth, what Earthlings call death, and he's now visiting with the Son. He'll shortly be here, and you'll see what occurs when a good spirit has completed his Earthly mission."

"What should I do while he's here?"

"Just observe and learn."

Quietly retiring to a nearby tree, Mathias waited. Instantly there was a feeling of energy, and the area near Brother Olvin got bright. Mathias was used to the feelings of peace that emanated from Superior Beings, but this was unusually strong.

Inside the all encompassing light he saw and felt the strength of the newly arrived spirit. Witnessing the enveloping love of the two spirits as the light from both of them merged, he enjoyed the ecstatic feelings of joy that spilled from the two spirits to him. For some moments there was only this awesome sense of adoration, peace, power, and loving reunion.

Mathias watched and felt of the euphoric feelings that radiated from Brother Olvin and Jim. He could feel and understood the

love and pride of Bother Olvin as he transmitted: *Welcome home,
Jim. We've been waiting for you with all our love.*

The adoration and wonder that Jim felt on seeing his father
were also felt by Mathias. These were pure feelings of bliss. He
was witnessing the renewal of a familial relationship that had been
broken by the earlier death of the father, and now, was regained by
the spiritual fourth birth of the son. Mathias marvelled as he
witnessed what was happening.

Still feeling of the love and joy that spilled from the two
spirits, Mathias was aware of a brief communication from Brother
Olvin to his son. *How's your mother, Jim. I miss her so, even
though she often communicates through prayer and I see her in
visions.*

*Mom's doing fine, Dad. She was going to come to Utah and
help Lori with the new baby. I thought I'd be helping also—I
didn't expect to be here so soon. My worry is for Lori.*

Lori's fine, son. Here, look!

Mathias watched as a vision unfolded that they could all see.
Bathing the baby was Martha Blair, Jim's mother, while Lori sat
in a nearby chair. Lori was saying: "Really, Mother Blair, I'm
very healthy. You got breakfast for the children, and now this.
You don't have to do everything."

Martha laughed, and commented: "I love being with you and
the children, Lori. California will be calling me home soon
enough, so just relax and enjoy it. It gives me an opportunity to
get closer to all of you. . . ."

The vision faded and Jim transmitted: *I'd forgotten how those
visions work. Thanks, Dad. It's wonderful to be home again with
the advantages that this life offers. Gravity can really be a pain at
times—not to mention injury and illness. What a relief it was to
leave my pain-filled body. Who was the guide who met me?*

*That was a distant cousin, Frank Blair. He's one of those
persons that Lori found during her research work on your genealogy. We taught him The Word, and he accepted it. You acted as
proxy for his temple work, and we thought it only proper that he be
privileged to serve as your guide. You didn't recognize him, then?*

At first I was overwhelmed by the realization that I was dead. When I saw my body lying in the truck and Roger trying to get me out, it didn't seem real. When the guide came, there was something familiar about him, but I wasn't sure what.

Signalling to Mathias to join them, Brother Olvin transmitted: *Jim, you need to meet Mathias. He's preparing for his Earth-birth, and he may choose to join our family—as the son of Alvin and Sue.*

Mathias felt himself embraced by the light of Jim. He responded with his own light, and he was conscious of the transmitted message: *What a splendid family you'll be joining, Mathias. Sue and Alvin have created a home of love and opportunity. You'll have a marvelous life.*

Feeling somewhat awkward, Mathias responded: *It's not certain, yet, that I'll be going. I must admit that it seems to be an attractive choice. There are others involved, though, so we shall see.*

Feeling the disappointment of Brother Olvin, Mathias decided to say no more. He waited for what might come next. Brother Olvin broke the silence with the transmission: *That's one of the reasons you're here, Jim, to help us teach Mathias about Earth.*

Mathias was shocked. Did Brother Olvin mean that Jim had been called back from Earth in order to help him? He was relieved to receive the next transmission from Brother Olvin, saying: *The main reasons that you were called home, though, had to do with your brother, Johnny, and with all of your ancestors that we need to teach. Many of them are those that Lori found in her genealogical research.*

What's the problem with Johnny, Dad?

Some of the vision-futures that I saw of him were pretty grim. Then, on our recent trip to Earth I was present when he was arguing with Alvin. It was a bad scene.

Brother Olvin continued, *Johnny won't admit it, even to himself, but his health isn't very good. He smokes and drinks far too much, and he has an ulcer. It appears that everything is soon going to come to a climax, and I think we three may be able to help him.*

Mathias was amazed at what Brother Olvin had said. Wondering how he would be able to help, he decided that he would do whatever Brother Olvin asked. His love for Brother Olvin was deepening.

❦   ❦   ❦   ❦

Completing his lecture for the upper division students of philosophy, Professor John Blair was dissatisfied. He never ceased to be amazed at the ignorance of his students—yet these Berkeley students at Cal were supposed to be a choice group. He wondered what the less-choice group must be like.

Having just finished lecturing on Nietzsche's "Thus Spake Zarathustra," Professor Blair had discussed Nietzsche's point that God was dead. He expanded on Nietzsche's consequent logic that the old verities of good and evil were no longer true. Some of his students seemed to appreciate the logic of Nietzsche's position, but too many of them, Professor Blair could tell, still believed in the folk-tales of their parents. A few of the students were as biased with religious superstitions as was his brother, Alvin.

Getting in his car, he was anxious to get to his home on Spruce Street, in the Berkeley hills. He enjoyed the privileges that his position and money gave him, but this morning, after listening to some of his students, his stomach began hurting again.

His stomach problem, he thought, must also be due to the argument that he and his wife Barbara had at breakfast. She was arguing for children, again. What was wrong with the way they were living, now, he wondered? Children would just intrude on their lifestyle. Most assuredly, a child would interrupt a portion of Barbara's career as a Professor of Law—and he had angrily pointed this out. Why did women always cry when you succeeded with a point of logic?

Driving into his garage, he climbed the steps to his house and struggled with the key. Finally managing to get the door open as another pain hit his stomach, he felt beads of perspiration on his brow. Rushing to the bathroom, he tried to get relief, without much success, so he took a couple of Zantacs and two Carafates.

Still feeling weak, he lay down on the living room couch so that he could relax.

Professor Blair decided that he would take a small Scotch to help him relax. His doctor had advised against alcohol, but this was a special circumstance. From experience he knew that alcohol reduced the pressures of life, and he certainly needed relaxation at this moment. The glass touched his lips and he felt the familiar warm glow as the alcohol did its soothing work passing into his troubled interior. Lighting a cigarette, and relaxing on the couch, Professor Blair already felt better. Now, he would just close his eyes for a brief period . . . yes, that was what would rejuvenate him, it was what he needed. . . .

Waking in a cold sweat, Professor Blair felt an immediate and overwhelming urge to throw-up. Barely making it into the bathroom in time, he violently regurgitated into the toilet and to his horror saw that much of the residue in the toilet was blood—his blood. After several minutes of violent retching, he cleaned himself somewhat and struggled to the telephone.

Barely reaching the telephone because of his dizziness and the ringing in his ears, he dialed his wife's office number. Hoping that she would be there, he waited as it rang. Relief went through him as he heard her voice. With difficulty, he said, "Barbara, I'm in trouble. I barely made it to the bathroom, and I vomited a toilet bowl full of blood. I'm not sure I can stay conscious."

The next two hours were a hazy blur to Professor Blair. He was vaguely aware that ambulance attendants lifted him onto a stretcher from the bathroom floor. The helicopter flight was a dim recollection of people sticking needles into him, and of the dull roar of the motor and rotors. The first really conscious moment was waking in the hospital room with Barbara sitting next to him.

Feeling great relief as her husband opened his eyes, Barbara tried not to show how concerned she had been. She kept her voice as calm as she could. "Well, Professor, you gave us quite a scare. Welcome back."

Professor Blair weakly asked, "What happened?"

"It was your ulcer, Johnny. Dr. Nielsen examined you as soon as you got here, and they pumped a lot of blood into you to replace what you lost. It's still critical, though, and that's why all the monitors are hooked to you."

Professor Blair looked at the monitoring machine and noticed two nurses standing nearby. "Can they give me anything for this pain? It's awful."

"They've already given you all that they can, John. Fortunately, they've stopped the bleeding, but Dr. Nielsen says they need to operate right away to prevent additional bleeding, and they don't want you too sedated before the operation. He's worried about your blood pressure."

"Why don't the fools get on with the operation, then?"

"They will as soon as they can, Johnny."

Her husband normally seemed so domineering, and so in control of every situation, so Barbara was astonished to see him conscious and yet looking so helpless with the tubes attached to him. She reached over on the bed and held his hand. When she did, she was even more surprised to see tears in his eyes. "John, it'll be all right."

"I hope so Barbara. I'm so terribly frightened."

"Don't be frightened, John. You'll have one of the best surgeons in the world working on you."

"It's just that I've never had to face my own mortality before. The possible idea of being extinguished is absolutely terrifying."

"Maybe we don't get extinguished when we die, John. After all, millions of people believe that there's a life after death. Even your own family . . ."

"I'm scared, Barbara, but I'm not stupid. No, when you die that's it. From dust to dust as the Bible says—and it's truly frightening."

"Well, your operation will fix you up like new. Then your fears will be over."

"Let's hope so. Where is that blasted doctor? The bums are never available when you need them."

"Please, John, that does not . . ."

Interrupting Barbara's comment was a high-pitched squeal from the monitor. The nurses looked startled, and one ran from the room.

With fear rising in her throat, Barbara glanced at John in time to see his eyes roll back in his head. He turned a gray color as she watched him. In a panicky voice the other nurse said, "You'll have to leave now, Mrs. Blair. Resuscitation people will be here any second."

Chapter 11

AN AMAZING EXPERIENCE

The next thing I knew I was standing looking at myself on the ground. . . . There was a sense of floating, and the realization that I must be dead. As part of my discovery that I was dead, I leaned close to my body and reached out to touch it. My hand, and it was a hand, went right through my body lying on the ground. It was a shock. [1]

To his surprise, Professor Blair found himself standing alongside of a hospital bed looking at his wife sitting with a frightened look on her face. Somebody was in the bed, and he asked her, "What's going on, Barbara?"

Squealing in the background was an annoying noise, and he heard the nurse ask his wife to leave. Asking his wife, again, what was happening, he became frustrated when she still did not respond. He shouted, "Damn it, Barbara, what the hell's happening?" She continued to ignore him, and she left the room as several doctors and nurses rushed in with a cart full of equipment.

Watching the medical people with some curiosity, he saw them pounding on the chest of the man in the bed. Looking at the patient, Professor Blair wondered who the sick person was. The poor bum looked terrible. Preparing to move closer, he heard

---

1 Gibson, Arvin S., 1924- , *Echoes From Eternity*, Published by Horizon Publishers, Bountiful, Utah, 1993, Story of Mike, pp. 154-155.

someone call his name. "John, come with us. Hurry, John, we'll help you."

Glancing in the direction of the doorway, he saw several shadowy forms motioning to him. They urged him, again, to follow them. The great pain he had been suffering had completely disappeared, so he decided to see who these people were.

Entering the hallway, Professor Blair was surprised to find himself in a dense fog. The people were ahead of him, though, and they were still calling, "Hurry, John. Follow us and it'll be all right."

Continuing for some distance through the fog, Professor Blair began to be concerned. He had no idea where he was or who these people were. Their pleading for him to follow them was even more urgent than it had previously been. He was tempted to break it off and return, except he did not know how to find his way back through the fog. To his dismay, it seemed to be getting darker.

Finally, Professor Blair decided that he would go no farther until he knew who these people were and where they were taking him. Besides, it was getting dark.

Pausing in the dark, the professor was horrified to realize that the people were beginning to attack him. Several of them climbed on him and began to scratch and bite him. Appalling growling noises escaped from them during the attack.

Attempting to defend himself, he struck back. This only intensified the attack as dozens more joined the fray. He felt his energy draining as multitudes of the awful beings attacked him. The more distressed he became, the greater seemed to be the pleasure of the offensive creatures.

As his energy was depleted, Professor Blair sank in despair into a collapsed and pitiful heap. He abandoned himself to whatever they would do to him, assuming that he would be obliterated. Lying in the increasing darkness, he noticed that the creatures seemed to lose some interest since he had given up fighting them.

In a state of complete abandonment to whatever fate would do with him, Professor Blair heard a voice—his voice. The voice said: "Pray."

Wondering at the voice, and in total collapse, he lay help-lessly, when the voice spoke again. "Pray." This time he responded, "I don't know how to pray." The voice spoke a third time, and again it demanded: "Pray to God."

Gathering what little strength he had left, the professor began to say "God help me. In God we Trust. Our Father which art in heaven . . ." and other sayings that had a churchy sound to them. To his surprise the beings surrounding him became extremely agitated. Backing away from him, they shouted "Stop it John! There is no God! Be quiet!"

Discovering his new weapon, Professor Blair continued to shout religious-sounding phrases until the terrible beings disap-peared. Completely drained of strength, and still feeling as if he were about to be annihilated, he waited for his eradication. Then he heard his own voice singing a song he had not heard since a small child. It was the little song *Sunbeam*: "Jesus wants me for a Sunbeam, . . ." and it kept repeating. Lying in complete darkness, and in total desperation, John called, with his last ounce of strength, "Jesus, please save me."

Suddenly, above him and at great distance, a small light appeared. Watching the light, he noticed that it was mov-ing—toward him. The light increased in size and brightness until the radiance enveloped him. Within the brilliance of the light, Professor Blair watched in astonishment as his torn body was mended by the healing power of the light. Lifted by the light, he felt himself being transported into space; stars were twinkling their eternal messages around him for as far as he could see.

Embraced by the light, Professor Blair found himself crying uncontrollably. The intense love that he was feeling was beyond anything he had ever experienced, and his emotions were difficult to control. With what control he could muster, he sobbed into the light, "Put me back . . . put me back in the darkness, I don't belong here."

The light answered, and for the first time Professor Blair was aware that it was talking into his mind as he heard it say: *No, Johnny. You belong here.*

Looking again into the light, three personages were visible. Their radiant glory was beyond belief. And there was a feeling of something . . . no, it was more than a feeling. There was a knowledge that he was coming home. He had been here before, and the people in the light, they were . . . he suddenly understood that his father and his brother were there. He communicated: *Dad?*

Caressed by the enormous love of the individuals in the light, he heard his father's voice in his mind: *Johnny, we love you, but you need to change. You've hurt others, and the Son, by some of your actions.*

Am I going back? John asked.

It depends on you, Johnny, his father responded. *Let's look at your life.*

Then, to Professor Blair's complete amazement, in the midst of space, and appearing before him as the ultimate video, in color, with three dimensions, stereophonic sound, and with feeling, his life rapidly played before him. In each event where he interacted with other individuals, or where what he did had an effect on others, he saw and felt the results of what had happened.

He saw many events in his youth where he had taken advantage of his two brothers to gain undeserved privileges over them, and he felt of their hurt. On another occasion, he saw and felt himself contriving to get even with his wife because she had not cancelled her teaching class in order to attend one of his many meetings. In his emotions he relived the feelings of anger with his wife, and he felt of her hurt when he succeeded in punishing her. Incident after incident unfolded before his eyes, and his guile and hypocrisies, as he saw them in their true light, were devastating.

When the vision of his life became too much for him to handle, the life-story stopped, and he felt of the love of those viewing it with him. Their abounding love gave him the courage to continue—and the vision continued.

In one terrible example, where he had cooperated with another professor on a lifetime research project, he saw himself take advantage of a portion of the other professor's work and claim the entire project for his own. An investigation followed, and he was awarded the rights, including copyrights, for the work that the professor had done. Some time later, the professor became an alcoholic and was dismissed from University employment. John felt again the greed of his own position—and then he felt the agony of the other professor and his family.

Throughout this ordeal, John could feel the hurt of others that he had misused, but he could also feel the disappointment of the beautiful spirits watching it with him. They did not say anything, but he could tell by their feelings when they disapproved of something he did. On those few occasions in his life when he did something solely for the benefit of others, he could feel the pleasure of the watching spirits at his success. One of the highlights of his life was when he came home from school as a teenager and helped his younger brother prepare for some scout merit badge tests.

The tangible nature of the love of those magnificent beings watching the life's review was what allowed John to get through it. Without them and their love it would have been too devastating. Upon completing the review, his father asked: *Do you have any questions?*

And John had a myriad of questions. He first asked: *What's going to happen to me?*

That depends on you Johnny. You will have some choices to make. But first, are there any other questions that you have?

Yes, I was such a fool. The depth of Johnny's anguish and embarrassment were difficult to endure, until he felt of his father's responding love. Johnny continued: *I was so sure there was no life after death. What is life over here like?*

Immediately he was transported to a different world. It was a world of lawns, trees, shrubs, some of which he had seen on earth, and many that he had not. The colors were beyond belief, much brighter and more dynamic than he had ever seen before—they seemed to have a life of their own. In the background was a sound; it was a sound as if a thousand voices were blended into a soft melody of indescribable beauty.

He found himself walking, or rather drifting, with his companions along a path, with many other happy beings, toward some buildings that glowed with their own light. The beings that he saw seemed intensely occupied with various pursuits in the buildings.

What're they doing, and what's the purpose of these buildings? John asked.

His father answered: *The buildings are the Libraries, and they contain all the information in the universe. The people are researching the knowledge that's there, and they're adding to it.*

So people have work and assignments in this life?

Absolutely, and that work can have overriding importance.

Why was Jim killed in the prime of his life?

People on Earth can die for any number of reasons, including unplanned accidents, illnesses, wars, and even murder brought about by evil persons. If that were not true, agency, which is so important for our progression, would be circumscribed. In Jim's case, however, it was different. Tell him, Jim.

Feeling of the great love of his brother, John became aware of the happiness that filled Jim. *I was called home, John, because I was needed more urgently here than on Earth. There are thousands of our ancestors who haven't been taught The Word, and I've been brought back to help Dad teach them. Their progression is stopped until they receive the Son in their lives. My wife, Lori, has been working on Earth to identify all our ancestors, and to see that their temple ordinance work is done.*

John asked: *So, then, what I was taught as a youth from the scriptures is true?*

Of course it's true, his father answered.

Why, when I read it as an adult, did it appear so full of contradictions?

Well, let's examine that portion of your life, again.

John saw himself researching the scriptures with a pile of books sitting on a table. His references were mostly philosophy books and other books with an anti-religion bias. As he researched particular passages of scriptures, he jotted down objections that corresponded to the knowledge he had obtained in his other references. His objective in the research, he now saw, was to prove the scriptures in error.

Transmitting a thought, his father began: *The scriptures, as you call them, are to be read prayerfully. They then reveal themselves to you easily. The Word will uplift, edify, and inspire you as you do that. And it'll reveal to you the truth—not the truth as men know it—but the truth as it's given by the Father and the Son.*

The questions continued to come from John, and as they did, his understanding expanded accordingly. Knowledge flowed into him from all directions, and it was knowledge that was familiar to him, as if he had opened a favorite book. Information was filling him from all sources, and it seemed that his body members, his eyes, his ears, his fingers, the very cells of his body were joyous receptors of this knowledge.

Finally, Brother Olvin transmitted: *You have a choice, Johnny, you may either stay here, or you may return to Earth.*

What happens if I stay?

If you stay, because of the way you lived, your progress will be limited. You will be taught The Word, and if you accept it, and I think you will, you'll receive a measure of glory. But, you will forever be plagued by the misuse of your time while you were on Earth—with the corresponding missed opportunities for your own growth.

And if I go back?

You'll have continued opportunities to prove yourself, just as you had before you came here, and there are no guarantees that you'll succeed. In fact, to restore much of your agency you'll forget a great deal of what you saw and were told here. You'll forget, for example, what you were told about the reasons for Jim's being called home. You'll remember only that which is necessary for your future development.

What will my future life on earth be?

It's largely up to you, Johnny. You can make of it what you will. Because you were privileged to visit the spirit world before the completion of your Earthly mission, however, your life in the future will be more difficult than it otherwise would have been. Certain physical difficulties and related pain will afflict you for much of your remaining life.

So, as they say on earth, I'm damned if I do, and damned if I don't. Johnny laughed as he thought of the two choices being offered him.

Brother Olvin smiled as he recognized the Earthly perspective in Johnny's comment. *In your first choice, if you accept The Word, you're only damned in the sense that your previous Earthly choices limited the progress that you can ultimately achieve in this realm. Through the atonement and mercy of the Son, though, the glory that you achieve will still be beyond anything you can imagine.*

Johnny suddenly saw in vision the glory of his future abode if he stayed, and it was glorious. He was entranced with what he saw.

If you return—depending upon how you live—it's possible that you can remove all limitations on your future growth. In that event these are a few of the blessings you may realize.

Standing near him, and to the side, Johnny saw two beautiful persons, a young man and a young woman. They smiled and he could feel familial love radiating from them. His brother's voice, in his mind, said: *These are your son and your daughter, Johnny.*

Choking on his emotions, Johnny next saw something that he did not understand. His brother communicated the thought that it could be part of his future on Earth, but John still did not know what it meant. Unfolding in vision was a large, white building sitting on a hill, with a tall central tower, and four smaller towers. Palm trees, flowers and lawn surrounded the building. Inside the building he saw people dressed in white and involved in some type of ceremony.

Still puzzling over the last vision, he next saw a view of what his future glory might be after the successful completion of his Earthly mission. He saw himself—and Barbara—and other family members, with power and glory that defied description. He understood that he was in a realm where the Son and the Father dwelt. The feelings of euphoria and love that filled his bosom were such that he never wanted to lose them.

Pondering what he had seen, heard and felt, John was startled as his father's voice, in his mind, intruded on his thoughts.

Johnny, I love you, and I always will regardless of which choice you make. It's time, now, to make your choice. What will it be?

And I'll always love you, Dad. Concerning the choice, though, I'm frightened that if I return to earth I'll repeat the bad choices I made before, or even worse. Will you and Jim be able to help me when I need you?

Of course, John, if you pray, and call upon the Father in the name of the Son, we can be assigned to come to Earth and help as needed. Just remember to read The Word, to pray, and to love your fellow beings.

Then, Dad, I choose to go back.

Are you sure?

Yes, I am sure.

Are you sure?

Yes, I think so.

Are you sure?

This time it hit John. His answer must be certain—he must not lie to himself or try to conceal the real intent from his father and his brother. He remembered, again, the two beautiful persons that could be his children. *Yes, I'm certain. I choose to return.*

Just before he lost all consciousness of the spiritual realm that he was in he heard his brother's voice in his mind. *Johnny, tell Lori that I'll always love her and that everything will be okay. And tell the children that we'll be together again. Don't forget, I'll love Lori forever, and everything will be fine.*

Waking to a terrible pain, Professor Blair looked around and saw that he was in a hospital bed. Sitting next to the bed, and holding his hand, was his wife, Barbara. His eyes fluttered, and he sighed.

"Thank the Lord you are back," said Barbara.

"Yes, I'm back, Barbara," John responded with great difficulty. "And it was because of the Lord that I'm here."

"What do you mean, John?"

"Its difficult to talk. I hurt all over, . . . and I'm so weak. But I had the most marvelous . . . it was an unbelievable experience. When I'm stronger I need to tell you about it."

"You can tell me later, John, when you're stronger. You hurt because they had to remove most of your stomach. Also, before the operation your heart stopped—while I was with you—and they almost lost you. There appears to have been some permanent damage to your heart, but they think, in time, you'll be able to resume your normal teaching load and research work. The University has been terrific. Professor Adams is temporarily taking your classes.

"For now, the doctors said that once you came out of the coma you were in, the most important things would be rest and your will to live. So, just rest, John. We can talk later."

"Everything will be fine, Barbara. I love you."

Her eyes filling with tears, since John rarely told her that he loved her, Barbara squeezed his hand. "I love you, John."

Two days later, John awakened feeling hungry. Barbara was sitting at his bedside, and he said: "I feel much better, Barb, do you think they could get me some breakfast?"

Ringing for the nurse, who seemed pleased with his request, Barbara said: "You look stronger. You were so weak when you first regained consciousness that we all worried about you. By the way, Alvin and Sue have been here to see you, and they spoke briefly to you. Do you remember their visit?"

"Not really. It's all sort of a blur. I remember you sitting here through most of my illness."

"Your mother called, and she was going to come out and visit, but I told her to stay where she was. She's still helping Lori cope with Jim's death. It seemed that she could do more good there than here. She promised to visit when you're better."

John was not too pleased with his breakfast, which he described as strained baby food, but he felt much stronger after eating. Lying back on his pillow, he said: "Barbara, I need to tell you what happened when I was so sick."

"You said, when you first came to, that you had an experience. I've been curious as to what you meant."

John was unsure of how to begin. His experience had been so real, and yet . . . what would Barbara think? He tentatively said: "It's just that things were so different from what I imagined. You'll think I was crazy."

"No I won't John. Please go ahead." Barbara reached for his hand and squeezed it as she attempted to give her husband confidence.

"Do you remember what happened when my heart stopped?"

"I'll never forget, it was one of the most frightening things I ever witnessed."

"Well, I watched you as the nurses made you leave the room."

"But, John. You were completely out of it. How could you see me?"

"That's just the point. I was out of it—out of my body, that is. My body was lying in the bed and you were by the side of me. I was above you looking down, only I didn't know at the time that it was my body in bed."

Barbara began to cry as she understood the implication of what John was saying. She reached over and kissed him on the forehead. "Go on, John."

"I actually died, and I went to another world. Dad and Jim were with me. Dad said I need to change the way I've been living."

Astonished at what John was telling her, Barbara struggled with her emotions. "What do you mean, you need to change the way you've been living?"

"My selfish desires have always driven me. I saw myself as others saw me, and it was dreadful. Love needs to become more a part of my life—love for everybody—but especially for you and the rest of my family. And Barbara, I saw our son and our daughter. At least they could be our children if we want them. They were beautiful."

Barbara's crying, which she had controlled with difficulty, resumed. After a few moments she regained her composure. "That must have been quite an experience. Do you feel up to telling me just what happened?"

John then proceeded to tell everything he remembered from his experience. Stopping at times to rest, and to regain control of his emotions, he exhausted himself telling the story. Upon completion of the story, both John and Barbara were in tears. "Barbara, I'm exhausted. May I sleep for a while?"

"Of course, my love. I'll be here when you wake."

Barbara ran some errands, and when she returned she found John sitting awake in his bed. Smiling a greeting to her, John seemed anxious for her to join him.

"Barbara, I talked with Dr. Jepson who was the principal physician on the resuscitation team that worked to revive me when my heart stopped. He confirmed that I was clinically dead for a short period, and he said they didn't think I'd be able to come out of it. If I did, they thought that I'd have severe brain damage because of the length of time I was gone."

"Do they think there still might be some brain damage?"

"Apparently not, and they're surprised. A neurologist ran some tests on me while you were gone, and I seem to test-out normally. They'll not know, for sure, until time has elapsed and I've exercised both my short- and long-term memory. For now, though, they're quite encouraged."

Barbara reached for his hand. "I will love and cherish you, Johnny, whatever the state of your memory."

Smiling through his tears, John said: "The really exciting news, though, was what I was able to confirm with Dr. Jepson. I told him that I saw him working on me during the resuscitation effort, and I could describe what the different team members were doing. At one point Dr. Jepson cursed when the nurse didn't inject some medicine into me properly, and she started to cry. When I described the situation, and other details, he was amazed. He said there was no way that I should have been able to see what they were doing since I was clinically dead. Once before, he said he had another patient that saw himself being worked on, but he didn't remember the detail that I did. Of course, at the time that I was witnessing this, I didn't know it was my body they were working on. I thought it was some other poor jerk." Johnny laughed as he remembered his feelings of pity for the body he saw in the bed.

"That's wonderful, Johnny. It confirms the reality of your experience, doesn't it?"

"It does for me. But then, I don't need proof. The experience was the most real thing I've ever undergone. It was more vivid and real than you and I sitting here and talking together. In fact, I've concluded that this world is the dream world. The other world, the one that I was in, is the real world. And it's home—this is only a temporary abode."

Barbara laughed. "If some of your professorial comrades could see you now. Several of them visited you when you were unconscious. What're you going to tell them?"

"I'm not sure. It depends on how I feel at the time." John laughed as he thought of his colleagues. "If I described the whole story, as I did for you, most of them would think either that I had gone bonkers, or they would attribute it to a drug-induced hallucination. It was neither of those things. When I was with my Dad and Jim, I was more alert than I've ever been in this life. And the peace . . . the peace, Barbara. It filled my entire being."

"You'll have to tell your family."

"That's right. When I'm better we should visit Mom and Lori and tell them about Jim and Dad. Also, I need to get together with Alvin and Sue and apologize for the way I treated Alvin at Jim's funeral. He was right, and I was wrong. My arrogance and pride were unbelievable."

Chapter 12

A DIFFERENT LIFESTYLE

The love I felt from Him during this period was extremely intense. Love traveled from my toes to my head, filling my entire body. . . . It was a fatherly type of love, and I knew that He was pleased when I acknowledged my sins and asked if I could amend for them. He held me in His arms the whole time, and the feelings were so intense. . . . While I was embraced by Him and felt of His great love, He asked me if I would help others to come back to Him. I said I would. [1]

Two weeks had elapsed since his release from the hospital, and John Blair was a different person. He was still dedicated to teaching philosophy at the University of California, but he had concluded that the main thrust of his lectures must change. No longer would John give a subliminal message that religion was for the uneducated and superstitious. Rather, his message would be of the importance of the brotherhood of man, and of the need for the unconditional love of all people.

John was not sure that he should embrace any particular religion, especially the religion of his youth, the LDS faith, with its emphasis on latter-day prophets. He suspected there were no such beings. Keeping an open mind, though, would be part of his

---

1 Gibson, Arvin S., 1924- , *Echoes From Eternity*, Published by Horizon Publishers, Bountiful, Utah, 1993, Story of Elizabeth Marie, pp. 171-172.

future thinking—he might even listen to his mother. Chuckling to himself, John wondered how his mother would react if he started listening to her.

John's health was still delicate, and probably always would be according to the doctors, but he knew from his spiritual experience that this was a necessary penalty for his return to earth. Bearing the associated pains and disabilities with serenity would be a major goal of his future life.

What a marvelous wife he had. And to think of how he had previously taken her for granted—worse yet, how he had dominated her life with his own selfish desires. Barbara had sacrificed her own career for his needs throughout much of his life. During his illness she had proven through her actions what a bedrock of strength she was. His nearly dormant love for her had rekindled into a blazing fire.

Staring at the turbulent San Francisco Bay as their car sped south on the freeway toward San Jose, John thrilled at the splendor of the scene. Sea gulls played their exhilarating dance in the sky as they squawked competitively at each other. Even the freeway, with its bustling cars and the silly sculptures in the Berkeley mud-flats, seemed to express the vitality of life. Why was it he had never noticed the beauty of his surroundings before this illness? What a dolt he had been.

Breaking into his reverie, Barbara asked, "Are you sure you feel up to this trip, John? We could postpone it until you feel stronger."

"I'm fine, Barbara. You're doing all the driving. Besides, I need to let Alvin and Sue know that I think enough of them to make a trip to their place. They came to the hospital and visited me several times and I hardly talked to them."

"You were too sick, John. They understood that."

"Sure I was sick, but it's time, now, to let them know that I love them. Also, I need to tell them about my experience."

"They'll be thrilled to hear of your experience."

Basking in the afterglow of an early afternoon dinner with Alvin, Sue and their two children, Barbara still could not believe how well it had gone. There was none of the tension that usually accompanied a visit between John and Alvin. It had helped, of course, that John hugged Alvin as soon as he saw him—and that he expressed his love for his brother. It was almost laughable to see the surprised looks on the faces of Sue and Alvin. Wiping the tears from their eyes, afterward, both John and Alvin launched into a discussion of Alvin's two growing girls.

Leah and Rose, Alvin and Sue's five- and three-year-old children, adjourned to the family room after dinner and the adults continued their conversation. "Those are wonderful children you have, Sue. Their energy seems endless," commented Barbara.

"You're right about their energy," laughed Sue. We'd like a boy to balance the thrust of their energy."

"Is this an announcement, Sue?" asked John.

"I'm not pregnant this instant," replied Sue, "at least I don't think I am." They all laughed, and she continued, "But, yes, we'd like to have another child."

There was silence for a moment, and then John spoke up, "So would we," in an almost hushed voice.

"What did you say, John?" asked Alvin.

"I said that we'd like to have some children," and he reached over and grabbed Barbara's hand. She smiled at him.

"How fantastic. We were beginning to wonder if you'd ever have children," commented Alvin.

"We probably wouldn't have if it hadn't been for my illness," said John.

"That's a strange comment. What did your illness have to do with having children?" asked Sue.

"It was an experience I had when I was ill—the most profound experience I have ever had."

"We knew you were very ill and almost died, Johnny," Alvin said. "Was that the experience?"

"In a way. At least, the illness led to the experience. According to the doctors, at one point my heart stopped and I was clinically dead. It was during that period that it happened."

"What happened?"

"I died, and during the period I was gone I had the most peculiar, the most dramatic, the most profound and real experience of my life. While I was in the other world I saw our future children, and they were radiantly beautiful."

Looking stunned, Alvin and Sue sat speechlessly for a moment. Alvin marvelled that it was his older brother that was telling him this—the brother who always doubted the existence of a life beyond this one. It must have been a remarkable experience to have this kind of an effect on John. Alvin softly said, "Tell us about it, Johnny."

Displaying more emotion than Alvin had seen in his brother since their youth, John proceeded to tell all that he remembered of his remarkable experience. It was an astonishing account, and they were moved by what John told them.

While John was telling his story, Barbara sat next to him, with tears in her eyes and holding his hand. She saw that Alvin and Sue were entranced by the story—they obviously believed John, and she loved them for it.

Completing the story, John looked somewhat drained.

"Are you okay, Johnny?" Alvin asked.

"I'm fine. It's emotionally demanding to tell you what I saw, felt and heard. Each time I do it I tend to relive portions of the experience. I needed to tell someone, though, besides Barbara, who would not think I was crazy."

"Have you told any others?" Sue asked.

"Only Barbara, and a portion of the experience to a couple of my physicians."

"Tell them what Dr. Jepson said," commented Barbara.

"Dr. Jepson was the primary physician who revived me. At first he was skeptical when I told him that I came out of my body— until I explained how I witnessed what he and the other members of the team were doing to me while I was clinically dead. There was no possible way that I should have been able to see them, he said. After my description, he believed me."

"I'm not surprised that he believed you, Johnny," remarked Sue. " I read one book, *Closer to the Light*, by Melvin Morse.

He told of many such incidents with children. They even have an acronym for your experience: *NDE*. It means Near-death Experience."

"There are several things about the experience that're puzzling, and I still don't understand them. My frustrations reach a peak at night when I try to remember just what everything meant."

"Such as what, Johnny?"

"Some of the things about Jim. I know that I saw both him and Dad, and I can remember almost everything that Dad said, except for something about Jim. It's almost as if I'm not supposed to remember something special about Jim. But I know we talked about him."

"Maybe it will come to you later."

"I think not. The other thing that bothers me, though, is that I don't understand part of the vision I saw of my future. It was the view I saw of the white building with towers. It seemed to be a strange thing to see, and I can't figure out what it meant."

"You really don't know what that meant, Johnny?" said Alvin as he winked at Sue. She smiled back at him.

"I have no idea. Do you?"

"I think so. Maybe we can show you. May we ride home with you in your car?"

❧   ❧   ❧   ❧

When they reached Oakland, Alvin turned off the freeway onto Fruitvale Avenue. They traveled up Fruitvale for some distance, then Alvin jogged onto Lincoln Avenue as it climbed into the Oakland hills.

Suddenly John erupted with excitement. "That's it, there it is!"

"That's what, Johnny?" asked Barbara.

"That's the building I saw in my vision—there, on the hill."

As they pulled into the parking lot surrounding the building, John saw palm trees, shrubs, lawns and flowers, identical to what he had seen during his experience. "Why, it's the Mormon temple, isn't it Alvin?"

"Yes, Johnny, it's the Mormon temple. We call it the Oakland Temple of The Church of Jesus Christ of Latter-day Saints."

"You knew it all along, didn't you? What a rascal you are."

"From your description, I was pretty sure that I knew what it was. I was only surprised that you didn't recognize it yourself. You must have seen the building many times from the freeway."

"Probably I did, but I was always preoccupied with being the busy professor. Besides, it's fairly far up on the mountain from the freeway."

"Would you like to go into the visitor's center?"

"May we?" asked Barbara.

"Yes. They encourage visitors to come in. The temple is restricted to worthy members of the LDS church, but the visitor's center is open to all who're interested."

"I'd like to see it, John. Do you feel up to it?"

"Yes. I'm curious, also."

Entering the smaller building next to the temple, they were met by an attractive young woman who introduced herself as Sister Goodfellow. She guided the group to a large white statue, explaining that it was a ten-foot marble copy of the Christus originally sculpted in the early 1800s by the Danish sculptor Bertel Thorvaldsen. As Sister Goodfellow described the features of the statue, Leah said: "That's Jesus, Mamma."

Sue hugged her daughter. "Yes, dear, that's Jesus."

Moving next, into what Sister Goodfellow called the Mountain Room with dramatic paintings of mountain scenes on the walls, the room was darkened and a thunder and lightening storm was simulated. Then, amidst the darkened clouds, a ray of sunshine beamed through, and the entire scene was likened to the storms of life with the light of the Savior providing a guiding light for all humans.

From the Mountain Room the group was led into a theater where either of two movies was shown. Due to limitations of time Alvin suggested that they watch only one of the movies, entitled

Together Forever. This was a very moving film which depicted the eternal nature of the family.

Leaving the visitor's center, and heading for the BART station, John broke the silence. "I think that I'd like to know more, if . . . if Barbara's interested."

Smiling, Barbara reached for John's hand. "I've always wanted to get some form of religion into our life, but you were so adamant against it, John, that I didn't think it was worth the trouble. Yes, I'd like to know more, too."

Barbara was thrilled with the prospect of again having religion in her life. As a child, she had been raised in a church-going Methodist family, and she missed the spiritual feelings that she had as a child. She had approached the subject a few times with John, but he had always been so violently opposed to religion—and so caustic in his remarks about anyone who practiced it—that she felt it would create too much trouble in her marriage for her to pursue it.

Looking worried, John said: "There's a problem, though." There was silence for a moment.

"What is it, John?" Alvin asked.

"Do you remember when I had my name removed from the LDS Church records?"

"I sure do. It nearly broke Mom's heart."

"Yes, and I was stupidly proud of what I did. Now, though, if I change my mind, will the church let me back in?"

Barely containing the excitement that he felt, Alvin said: "The Lord's church is not a punitive church, Johnny—it reflects the love of the Savior. It's the same love that you felt when you were in the presence of Dad and Jim."

"Yes, but . . ."

"No buts about it. Each of us are sinners, and without the mercy and redemption of the Lord, we'd all be lost. Through repentance and baptism both you and Barbara may receive all of the Lord's blessings."

"What should I do, Alvin?"

"From what you've said, both of you are interested in learning more of the church. Is that correct?"

After looking at Barbara, who nodded, yes, John responded in the affirmative.

"Then, I'd recommend that you have the LDS missionaries call on you. They'll teach you, in a series of lessons, what we believe. They'll give you material to read, and they'll answer your questions."

"Is that all there is to it?"

"I'd consider it a privilege to give your name to the missionaries. And I'll find out the name of the bishop in your area. You should probably make an appointment and let him know what you'd like to do."

"Thanks, Alvin. And, Alvin . . . "

"Yes, Johnny?"

"I love you."

Alvin was was thrilled with Johnny's message of love—the same message he had given Johnny following their argument after Jim's funeral. He had not retained any bitterness from their argument, but he had also not expected Johnny to ever respond with a message of love.

Chapter 13

A GIFT OF HOPE

The light of God rests on the face of brook and flow'r and
*   tree*
And kindles in our happy hearts the hope of things to be.
The light of faith abides within the heart of ev'ry child;
Like buds that wait for blossoming, It grows with radiance
*   mild.*
Today thine unseen purposes by faith's rare light we feel.
Dear Father, make us pure in heart; To us thy will reveal.[1]

Bathing Jimmy in the sink was pure pleasure for Lori. The baby's happy gurgles were as music to her ears. This was one chore that she performed herself, despite Mother Blair's willingness to do almost any work that Lori relinquished.

The help, and emotional support, that she had received from Mother Blair were of inestimable value. Staying for an entire month, Lori knew, was difficult for her, but she had never faltered. On occasion, after a busy day, Lori noticed that Mother Blair showed her age as she sank, exhausted, into an easy chair.

The telephone call from Barbara, assuring Mother Blair that there was no necessity for her to visit John while he was in the hospital, had reassured them all. Yet Lori knew that Mother Blair

1 Cahoon, Matilda Watts, 1881-1973, *Hymns of The Church of Jesus Christ of Latter-day Saints*, Published by The Church of Jess Christ of Latter-day Saints, Salt Lake City, Utah, 1985, p. 305.

worried about her professor son. One follow-up letter from Barbara made clear that John had been very seriously ill—near death, in fact. That is what made the recent phone call from John seem so strange.

Talking to John, after he spoke with his mother, Lori had never heard him sound so enthusiastic about a visit to Utah. She appreciated that he was trying to be kind to her because of the loss of her husband, but still . . .?

An ostensible purpose of the visit was to bring Mother Blair home on the same airline when John and Barbara returned to Berkeley. Their agreement to stay for several days in Lori's house, and to sleep in the back bedroom, though, was unheard of. John, or Professor Blair as he preferred to be called, *always* stayed in the best hotel available in Price—on the few occasions that he visited them.

Even more puzzling were Barbara's comments on the telephone. Since Professor Blair's marriage to a fellow professor, Lori had only seen Barbara two or three times. Barbara always seemed so occupied with her professional career that she didn't seem to have time for John's family. She was polite enough on the few occasions they'd been together, but there was never any closeness. In the recent telephone conversation, however, she sounded eager to visit and see the new baby.

Hoping that everything would work out during their visit, Lori wondered about the wisdom of her offering to have them stay in the house. She'd never expected them to accept. Especially troubling was the fear that religious conflicts would intrude. She and Mother Blair, for example, had family prayer with the children, and on Monday nights they held family home-evening with a religious lesson. Finally, there was church on Sunday, and since the visitors were arriving on Saturday, and staying through Wednesday, Mother Blair, the children and Lori would be going to their meetings.

Then there was John's smoking. He seemed addicted to his cigarettes, and he was always miserable, they all knew, when he couldn't smoke in their presence.

Mother Blair and Lori were nervously fussing in the kitchen when the car drove up on their driveway. The front door banged open as Jeff came crashing in with the announcement: "They're here Mom."

"All right Jeff, go help them with their bags. See if Uncle John needs any special help. He's been very ill."

Jeff ran out and came struggling back with two large bags. Following him was Barbara, looking just as tailored and sophisticated as Lori remembered. The shock, though, was John. When he'd visited during Jim's funeral, he'd been his usual slightly overweight self. He must have lost fifty pounds, or more, and he looked so frail. Lori was afraid that he was going to fall as he tripped on the entrance rug.

Barbara embraced Mother Blair, then Lori. "How lovely everything looks. It's so nice to see you both, again."

Subduing her shock at John's appearance, Lori said, "We're so delighted that you came. Jeff will put your bags in the spare bedroom."

"Will that put you out?" Barbara asked.

"Not at all. The baby sleeps in my bedroom, and Mother Blair will join me in our bed."

Barbara seemed somewhat anxious. "Would it be okay if John took a nap on the couch? The trip was harder than he thought it would be."

Smiling weakly John embraced his mother and Lori. "Barbara watches over me as though I were one of her children—and I might as well be for all the help I am to her. She does all the driving now. I'll be all right if I can just rest for a period."

Trying to hide her surprise, Lori said, "Why, of course you may lie on the couch and rest. Alice, go get one of the large pillows from my bedroom."

"Thanks Lori. If I could just rest for awhile . . . rest seems to help. The others of you go ahead with lunch."

Adjourning to the kitchen, Lori had Alice bless the food, and she passed sandwiches to the children and to Barbara. She was about to say something, when Ruth, her youngest, asked, "Is Uncle John very sick, Mama?"

"He's been very ill, dear."

"Will he die like Daddy did?"

Lori was mortified, as she glanced at Barbara, who, surprisingly, smiled and reached to hold Ruthie's hand. "No, dear," Barbara said, "Uncle John's not going to die."

An awkward silence persisted for a moment, interrupted by a worried looking Mother Blair. "Johnny does look quite ill, Barbara. I hope this trip isn't too much for him."

Smiling reassuringly, Barbara responded, "An hour or so rest in the afternoon seems to restore John's strength. I'm sure he'll be fine. As to the trip, though, John insisted on it. He said that it was time for him to show his love for his mother, and to bring a special gift for you and the children, Lori."

Mother Blair's eyes were filled with tears, and she was unable to speak. Lori, after overcoming her initial surprise, said: "John didn't need to go to the trouble of bringing a gift back here just to help us, especially when he's been so ill. It's been a struggle since Jim's death, but we're managing okay."

"This is a unique gift from John to you and the children, Lori. He wants to give it to you on Sunday, and when you understand more of what he has to offer, I'm sure you'll want the gift."

"On Sunday? I suppose that'll work out in the afternoon. In the morning, Mother Blair, the children and I will be going to church. You and John can have a leisurely time in the house while we're gone."

"Actually, Lori, if John feels up to it, we'd like to join you in Sacrament meeting."

Neither Mother Blair nor Lori could say anything; they were too taken by astonishment. Watching them react to her announcement, Barbara could barely restrain a smile. "John and I have been taking the missionary lessons in preparation for our baptism into the LDS church. Hasn't Alvin told you about it?"

Making a poor attempt to conceal her surprise, Lori said: "Alvin? No, he called to see how Mother Blair and I were doing, but he said nothing about you, except that John was improving in health."

"Good. He promised not to say anything.   We wanted to surprise you."

Surprise was an understatement. Shock would be a better word. Lori could scarcely believe her ears. Mother Blair sat in stunned silence, afraid to say anything for fear that Barbara might change her mind.

"Well, surprise us you did," Barbara said.   "And what a wonderful surprise it is. We shall be delighted to have you join us in our church services."

꘎   ꘎   ꘎   ꘎

Lori was pleased with the way the morning had gone. John seemed much stronger after a good night's sleep, and he'd been eager to join them in Sacrament meeting. The meeting was a good one, centered on the theme of Christ's earthly mission, and, for a change, all of her children were reverent.

Returning from the meeting, they'd enjoyed a light lunch, and then John excused himself to take a short nap. He and Barbara continued to exude an air of mystery, and Lori was becoming intensely curious about the nature of the promised gift. She wouldn't have long to wait, since John promised to bestow it when he awakened.

It was 3:00 p.m., and John seemed much refreshed from his nap. Gathering the family in the living room, as John requested, Lori and the others expectantly waited.

"This is one of the hardest things I've ever done," John began, "yet I believe it will be one of the choicest gifts I can give you. It's a gift of hope, and it'll add to the gift of faith which all of you possess in abundance.

"You're aware that I was recently very ill. Actually, according to the doctors at U.C. Medical Center, for a period I was clinically dead. During that period I had the most unusual, the most profound, the most real, and the most marvelous experience of my life. The experience was unique.

"While the doctors labored to preserve my life, I found myself outside my body."

Lori showed some surprise as John began his story, but Mother Blair merely nodded her head in affirmation. She was aware of several such incidents she had heard of concerning early church pioneers.

John continued: "While I was out of my body, I was accosted by aggressive spirits who seemed dedicated to destroying me. When I understood what was happening, it was horrifying.

"Then, just as I'd abandoned myself to complete obliteration by these awful beings, I was instructed by a voice to pray. As I attempted prayer, for the first time in decades, the awful spirits left and a light came down and embraced me. In the light were three radiant beings.

"The amount of peace and love that I felt emanating from the three beings was beyond earthly description. Everything about them was love. While basking in the glow of their love, I suddenly became aware that I knew them—at least two of them. One of them, the one that seemed to have extraordinary power and authority, was . . . he was Dad." John could hardly continue as he looked at his mother. "He was Dad, Mom."

Mother Blair began to cry, and John had great difficulty continuing. "The second person standing in the light was, . . ." John paused to look at Lori holding her baby, "he was Jim."

Lori began to sob, and Mother Blair moved next to her and put her arms around her. The children were all sitting with wide eyes, and Alice, the nine-year-old, asked, "Was my Daddy with Jesus, Uncle John?"

"When I saw your Daddy, I think he'd already been to see Jesus, Alice."

Attempting to stem the flow of tears, no one said anything for several moments. Then John continued with his story until he had completed as much of it as he remembered. Lori had several questions.

"What did Jim look like, John?"

"He was dressed in a white robe, and it glowed, . . . no, everything about him glowed. He appeared to be about the same age as when I saw him last. In fact, Dad also appeared to be a young man. They were beautiful, just beautiful."

"Do you know who the other man was that you saw with Dad and Jim?" asked Mother Blair.

"At the time it seemed that I knew him, but I can't remember who he was. There was just a familiarity about him—or maybe it was an understanding that he was someone important to me. I don't remember any more than that."

"Speaking of remembering," said Lori, "you mentioned that Dad told you something important about Jim. Can you recall anything else about what it was?"

"No. In that particular instance, it's almost as if I were forbidden from remembering what it was I was told. I only know that it seemed very important at the time, and it was about Jim. Maybe it was . . . ?"

"What?"

"I was just trying to remember whether it was Jim telling me about himself, or Dad telling me about Jim. As I remember, it was Dad talking about Jim. Only he really was not speaking orally. It was mind-to-mind communication, and it was better than talking."

"How was it better, Johnny?" asked Mother Blair.

"The knowledge I received was more understandable. When they expressed themselves, I could hear their voices in my mind—and I knew that they could hear mine. It was instantaneous and it was perfectly clear; there was no confusion as so often is the case here."

"You said that you had many questions that were answered while you were there. Do you remember what they were?" asked Lori.

"There were many questions I had about what happens after death, what people did on the other side, how my life stacked-up against how I should've lived, what would happen if I chose to come back, how the earth was created, . . ."

"You had questions about how the earth was created?"

"I'll say I did—and how reality fit with what the scriptures said."

"Did you get an answer?"

"There were answers to all my questions. Anything I wanted to know, Dad seemed to delight in showing the answer. It was pure knowledge flowing from him into me. The process was simply amazing, and as intelligence poured into me it was as if I said to myself: 'Of course, I knew that all along.' Everything seemed familiar. It was like I was coming home to a feast of knowledge."

"Can you tell us what you learned about the creation?"

"No. Only that I learned that the scriptures are true, if you use them properly, and if you pray to have the truth revealed to you."

Jeff had been quietly listening to his uncle. During a pause in the conversation, twelve-year-old Jeff timidly asked, "Uncle John, did Dad say anything about us?"

Startled by the question, John enthusiastically responded, "He most certainly did, Jeff. Thank you for reminding me. The last thing I heard before I returned was your Dad saying, 'Tell Lori that I'll always love her and everything will be okay.' He also said, 'Tell the children that we'll be together again.' The message seemed to be a very important one, and one that Jim didn't want me to forget. He repeated it at least twice."

Lori began to cry again, and Jeff went to his mother and put his arm around her. "It'll be okay, Mom," he said. "Dad promised."

Chapter 14

A DECISION

Lead, kindly Light, amid the encircling gloom;
Lead thou me on!
The night is dark, and I am far from home;
Lead thou me on!
Keep thou my feet; I do not ask to see
The distant scene—one step enough for me. . . .
And with the morn those angel faces smile,
Which I have loved long since, and lost awhile.[1]

Meeting at their favorite location, on the top of Mount Isaiah, Laura and Mathias had completed their Quiets. Kolob-Star had broken the horizon, and Laura was thrilled by the view as she anticipated another rotation of Kolob-1 with the opportunities that would bring. This would be a special rotation since she would be with Mathias.

Mathias, too, was excited to be with Laura again. Since their trip to Earth together, Mathias had been busy with Brother Olvin, and he suspected that she had been occupied with Brother Parley. His signal to Laura was that they should meet on Mount Isaiah and review the status of the progress of each of them.

The biggest excitement for Mathias, though, was his decision to go to Earth. He now knew that, no matter what, he was

---

1 Newman, John Henry Cardinal, 1801-1890, *The Pillar of Cloud—Lead Kindly Light,* 1833, stanzas 1, 3.

committed to life on Earth. He could hardly wait to break the silence and tell Laura.

Finishing their prayers, Mathias began. "Thank you for coming, Laura, I have so much to tell you . . . and I have missed you terribly."

Embracing Mathias in the glow of her love, Laura said: "My thoughts have often been with you, Mathias. I hope you received them."

"I did, Laura, and I was grateful. Most of the time I've been with Brother Olvin, and he's taught me some amazing things about Earth." Mathias then proceeded to explain how he had participated in the near-death experience of John Blair, and how that experience had taught him a great deal about life on Earth.

"How exciting, Mathias. I can imagine what a thrill it must have been. I've never had anything like that happen to me."

"What've you been doing since we last met, Laura?"

"Brother Parley and Sister Thankful have been using me to help with many who have completed their Earthly missions. It was wonderful associating and working with such advanced spirits. I learned some of the techniques of creation."

"What do you mean, you learned the techniques of creation?"

"It has to do with faith and with The Word. In Matthew's writings for the History, he describes one event with the Son where Jesus rebuked his disciples for not being able to cast out devils. In explaining to them why they were unable to succeed where Jesus had, he said: 'Because of your unbelief: for verily I say unto you, If ye have faith as a grain of mustard seed, ye shall say unto this mountain, Remove hence to yonder place; and it shall remove; and nothing shall be impossible to you.' Brother Parley showed some of the spirits, and me, how that works."

"What did he show you?"

"See Jeremiah Peak next to us?"

"Yes."

"And do you notice the depression in the Moses Range, just beyond Lake Jacob?"

"Yes, I do, Laura. Why . . .?"

"Watch them carefully."

Hardly believing his eyes, Mathias watched as Jeremiah Peak suddenly appeared on the Moses Range. The characteristic features of Jeremiah Peak were clearly visible where previously there had been a depression in the Moses Range, and where Isaiah Mountain had previously had two distinct peaks, Jeremiah and Ruth, now there was just one.

Struggling with his senses, Mathias sputtered: "But, it was there a moment ago. How . . .?"

"Yes, Mathias, your senses are telling you the truth. The Jeremiah Peak has been moved. It was done by the power of The Word, through faith. That's what Brother Parley taught some of us. It's more difficult to accomplish on the physical Earth than it is in this spiritual realm, but the principle is the same."

"I knew," said Mathias, "from Teacher Gallexus, that we'd ultimately have the power to command the elements, as the Son did during his Earthly ministry, but I'd never seen it demonstrated before. Won't you get in trouble by moving mountains around in that manner?"

Laughing, Laura said: "Yes. Brother Parley might not be pleased if he thought I was using the power frivolously. When I moved it, though, I made sure that any life forms on the peak and in the depression would be accommodated in the move. Let's put it back where it was originally organized."

Watching closely, Mathias saw Jeremiah Peak restored to its familiar place on Mount Isaiah. The depression on the Moses Range returned.

"The whole point," continued Laura, "of Brother Parley's teaching the advanced spirits how to control the elements was so that, as they assume positions of priesthood authority, they'll be able to assist in the creation process—just as Elohim, Jehovah and Michael did for Earth."

"What about you, Laura? Why did he teach you?"

"Primarily because of my role as the mother of a prophet. Barnabas was also present during the creation lessons. And, Mathias, he's a marvelous spirit."

"He'd have to be to accept the calling of being a prophet. It seems reasonable to me that, as a prophet, he'd be taught how to control the elements. After all, Moses performed many miracles by calling on the Father and the Son when he freed the Israelites from the Egyptians. In fact, he parted the Red Sea so that they could escape Pharaoh's army. But I still don't see why you were taught the same things."

Sensing a touch of jealousy in Mathias, it surprised Laura. She extended her love, and she carefully chose her next words: "In the nurturing capacity as a mother I'll need to help my child develop his full potential. I'll not be called upon, directly, to exercise control over the elements, and in fact I'll forget on Earth much of what I was shown. But my faith in my child, and in the gifts he receives from the Father and the Son, must be real."

Listening to Laura, Mathias recognized his own weakness—that of wounded pride. But more important than his damaged pride, deep within himself Mathias had to face the situation as it really was—Laura was substantially ahead of him in her progress.

Moving mountains! He couldn't even make decisions for himself, much less move mountains. He loved Laura with everything that was in him, but if he continued to bind himself to her future she would necessarily have to slow to his pace. There was no way that he could match her pace—she was out of reach in so many different ways. It wasn't fair to her or to him for them to continue struggling on the same course.

Shielding his thoughts from Laura with difficulty, Mathias agonized over what he must do next. How could he tell his beloved that they should go their separate ways?

Despite Mathias's attempt to shield his thoughts, Laura sensed his inner turmoil. "What is it, Mathias?"

"Well it's just that . . . maybe . . ."

"Come on, Mathias. What are you trying to say?"

"What would you think if we each accepted different missions?"

Overcoming her shock, Laura paused in her thoughts. Was Mathias saying that he wanted to break off their long-standing commitment to each other. Did he now want to go to Krasak-3 instead of Earth? Was he telling her that he felt trapped by her attempting to mold him in a certain way?

"Are you saying that you don't want to go to Earth?"

"No, actually I wanted to meet with you to tell you that I had decided to commit to Earth. The council has asked that I appear before them, and I am ready to tell them I want to go to Earth."

"That's wonderful, Mathias. Are you saying, though, that we should no longer try to find our life together on Earth?"

"Yes, sort of. What do you think, Laura?"

Trying to shield her own thoughts from Mathias, Laura pondered his question. It was true that Brother Brigham had said that if Mathias could not keep up with Laura's pace she should find another candidate. She understood that Mathias occasionally reached a near trauma-crisis over some of the choices that he had to make. Perhaps she should remove some of the pressure on him, at least for a while.

"Would you feel better, Mathias, if we weren't so firmly bound to each other—until we saw how things developed?"

Would he feel better? He would feel miserable at the thought of possibly losing Laura, and yet . . . maybe if there weren't so much pressure. Why did everything have to be so hard?

"Yes, I think that might be the right thing to do."

❦   ❦   ❦   ❦

Entering the room where the council had convened, Laura and Mathias were greeted by the members of the council. Brother Brigham was at the head of the table, and sitting to his left were Brother Parley and Sister Thankful. Across from the Pratts were many Blairs. Brother Olvin Blair and Jim Blair were sitting on the right hand of Brother Brigham. Near the end of the table was Barnabas.

Brother Brigham urged Mathias and Laura to sit at the opposite end of the table. After offering a prayer, Brother Brigham began by requesting that everyone speak orally since they were making decisions concerning Earthly matters. "Many of you on this council speak highly of Sister Laura and Brother Mathias.

As you know, Sister Laura has accepted a calling to be the mother of a prophet, and Brother Barnabas has accepted a calling as a future prophet on Earth, Laura's son.

"We're convened today, at Mathias's request, to consider whether Mathias should receive the call to be the prophet's father. Before we do that, however, we need to receive a commitment from Mathias as to where he chooses to spend his birth-life. At one time, Mathias, you were considering both Earth and Krasak-3. Have you decided where you want to go?"

"Yes. I'm committed to a life on Earth."

Brother Brigham asked Mathias two more times if he was truly committed to Earth, and after receiving an affirmative response, said: "That decision is now made. Let's move to the more weighty question of whether or not a call should be extended to Mathias to be the father of a prophet. Does any member of the council have a comment concerning this issue?"

Mathias signalled a comment and was acknowledged by Brother Brigham. "My love for Laura is beyond measure, and because of that love I want the council to make a decision that will help her. In that regard, I'm not sure . . ."

"Go ahead, Brother Mathias."

"I'm not sure that I would be the best person to be her husband. I may retard her progression."

Feeling the mixed emotions of Mathias, Brother Brigham asked, "Sister Laura, since you'll be the mother of the prophet, how do you feel about Brother Mathias as the father of your child?"

"Mathias and I've been friends and companions, and we've shared love for each other, since the great war. We worked together in helping the Son rid our spiritual world of Lucifer and his followers. My hope, since The Plan was revealed, was to share Earth-life with Mathias.

"We have talked about it together recently, though, and it may be well . . . Could we leave the issue open—dependent upon how we both react to Earth life?"

Pondering what Mathias and Laura had said, Brother Brigham looked for further comments. Signalling a comment, Jim Blair was recognized. "When my brother, John Blair, visited us during his illness, Mathias was present. I could feel of his love and sympathy for my brother, even though he didn't know him intimately. Brother Mathias has great capacity for devotion and empathy for others. Those are wonderful characteristics for a father to have. It'd be marvelous, in my opinion, to have Mathias as a nephew."

"Those are, indeed, admirable attributes to have for the calling we're considering. Thank you, Brother Jim, for your comment. Brother Parley, you have something you'd like to say?"

"Yes, Brother Brigham. Although Brother Mathias would only be related to the Pratt line through marriage, and I'm not as directly affected as some others of the council, I'm still vitally interested in how he might measure up to such a call. If his performance as a father were to be sub-par it could seriously jeopardize the calling of Brother Barnabas. My concern relates to Brother Mathias's inability to make quick decisions. Would the discouragements of Earth be too much for him to handle?"

"That, too, is a legitimate concern. Sister Thankful, you appear to have a thought."

"The trials of Earth are surely a concern—goodness knows I had my share when I was there. But the issues of love for others, understanding the feelings of others, sympathy for the downtrodden, are overriding issues. And Brother Mathias has these gifts in abundance. He'd do just fine as the father of a prophet."

"Mathias, you've heard these comments. Do you have anything else you'd like to add?"

"I'm appreciative of all of the remarks, including the comment by Brother Parley. The problems of Earth *have* been disconcerting to me—sufficiently so that until recently I was not willing to make a commitment to go there.

"With the help of many, however, and especially Brother Olvin, I've been able to see Earth in a new light. My understanding has improved immensely concerning how the problems of Earth actually can be positive factors in building character. The difficulties of Earth can also contribute to negative traits, if we let the difficulties overwhelm us. The conflicts of Earth, and how they mold our personalities, provide a measure of our own growth and development.

"Earth's still a frightening place to me, but it's also a fabulous place. There's nothing to compare with Earth when it comes to freedom of choice and opportunities for testing our mettle. I hope and pray that mine is up to the challenge.

"I love Laura with everything that's in me, and I'd do nothing consciously to hurt or retard her development. For that, and for other reasons, I'll be completely supportive of the decision of this council. If you decide that I shouldn't have the calling as father of a prophet, then I'll understand and agree with the decision.

"My decision to go to Earth, however, is unequivocal. I've made up my mind to commit to Earth and that won't change independent of what the council decides.

"Thank you for even considering me for such a calling. May the Father bless you in your decision and in all else that you do."

There was silence for a moment. Then Brother Brigham asked, "Are there any other remarks or concerns about calling Brother Mathias to be the father of a prophet?"

Signalling a comment, Sister Thankful said, "Perhaps Sister Laura's suggestion would work. It might be best to leave the issue open concerning whether or not Mathias should be the father. We could provide spiritual support for him, and then, depending upon how he reacted, he could be chosen. If he didn't measure up, then someone else would fill the calling."

Sensing support from the council for Sister Thankful's proposal, and not sensing other comments, Brother Parley said: "All in favor of extending the provisional calling of Father of a Prophet to Brother Mathias—depending upon how he responds to Earth and to our spiritual support—please indicate by the raised hand." All but one of the hands went up.

"Are there any opposed to extending the call to Brother Mathias? If so, please indicate by the same sign."

Brother Parley raised his hand.

"Do you have anything to add to what you've already commented on, Brother Parley?" asked Brother Brigham.

"No. My concerns have been expressed. The council should know, however, that despite my negative vote I'll support the decision of the council, and my hopes and prayers will be with Brother Mathias."

"Thank you Brother Parley. The provisional call is then extended, Brother Mathias. From your previous comments I take it that you accept the calling?"

"Yes, Brother Brigham. And my thanks to the council. I understand the conditional nature of the call, and I shall do my utmost to justify your confidence in me."

"I'm sure that you will. Now if you'll allow us we'll set you apart to the calling. Brethren holding the Melchizedek Priesthood please join me. Brother Parley, would you pronounce the blessing?"

Listening carefully to the words, and feeling the strength of the collected brethren, the promises burned into Mathias's consciousness. He was assured that his righteous prayers would be heard and answered. Assistance from assigned angels, contingent upon his living righteously, was promised—to help Mathias through life's problems. He received assurance that the light of the Son and the influence of the Holy Ghost would be his. Most importantly to Mathias, he was told that dependent upon how he responded to life's challenges, incidents on Earth, prompted by spiritual beings, would lead him to his choice companion, Laura.

Chapter 15

THE GREAT ADVENTURE BEGINS

Know this that every soul is free,
To choose his life and what he'll be
For this eternal truth is given
That God will force no man to heaven [1]

Mathias could scarcely believe his good fortune. Finally, he had made the decision to go to Earth. Most importantly, though, he still could be Laura's husband. It was true that his performance on Earth must measure up to the provisional calling in order for him to be the father of a prophet, but at least the opportunity was still there. If, now, he could just live up to his own potential. He must learn to overcome his fears and self-doubts.

There was still one more major hurdle that he must overcome; namely, the choice of the final conditions for his birth at his pre-birth conference. Laura must make her choices also, but Mathias suspected that she had already decided on most of them. In Mathias's case, that wasn't true. In many areas he was uncertain as to what choices would enhance his prospects for success.

One of his weaknesses, for example, he knew was his propensity toward pride. Often, when he succeeded in accomplishing some difficult task, he found himself assuming a self-congratulatory posture instead of recognizing the help he'd received from others and from the Spirit.

---

1 Stephans, Evan. *Know This, That Every Soul is Free.* Hymn, 1835.

150

Perhaps his biggest weakness, he thought, was his occasional jealousy of the more advanced state of Laura. When he measured his own progress against that of Laura he often came up wanting—and his feelings about Laura and himself under these conditions were not healthy. This, too, showed him that his pride continued to be a stumbling block. Instead of rejoicing about the advanced state of Laura he found himself, too often, agitated because he was not equivalently endowed.

From his teachers, Brother Gallexus and Brother Olvin, Mathias understood that some of the final choices that spirits made prior to birth-life would either help them or hinder them in their eternal progression, depending upon how well the spirits understood themselves. Those choices, therefore, should be carefully made, and each individual should be aware of his or her own strengths and weaknesses. In some instances, where the individuals were not very advanced, it could be just as well to have advanced spirits make the choices for the person, or even to leave some of the possible choices to chance.

Mathias would use his remaining Quiets to help him relax his troubled spirit. It seemed that his spirit had always been turbulent, even going back to the great war. He had been one of the first to volunteer to help the Son. His enthusiastic spirit, so Laura had said, was one of the things that had attracted her to him. He must not, therefore, calm his spirit too much—he chuckled to himself as he thought of how hard he tried to please Laura.

One important factor that would help him to make the right choices in his pre-birth conference was the blessing he'd received for his calling. Those were enormous promises that had been pronounced on his head by Brother Parley, and he knew that he could draw on them. It was strange, but in this particular instance he seemed to be ahead of Laura. For some peculiar reason she'd not been set apart or received a blessing for her calling.

Pondering some of these issues, he was about to close his Quiet with a prayer when he received a transmission from Laura: *Mathias, Beloved, please come to our favorite location, now. It's urgent that you join me.*

Arriving at the familiar spot on Mount Isaiah, Mathias spotted Laura. Also present were Brother Brigham, Brother Parley and Brother Olvin. Wondering why such an auspicious group was gathered, Mathias extended his love to each of them, and especially to Laura. She responded and then transmitted: *Mathias, the most wonderful thing, I was told . . .*

At that moment the atmosphere, which normally on Kolob-1 enjoyed a nominal energy field, seemed to be building to some unusual climax. Light, brighter than that from Kolob-Star, was streaming into the spot where they were standing. The shrubbery, the trees, the flowers, even the rocks seemed to be a part of the energy field which continued to build. In fact, the very atmosphere appeared to be rejoicing in a euphony of praise.

Mathias was jubilant with the feelings that swelled within him. All doubt, concern, worry, fear, and anxiety were replaced with euphoria, joy, bliss, love, knowledge, and peace—overwhelming peace. He never wanted to lose these feelings.

Wondering at the splendor of his feelings, Mathias was astounded when suddenly a glorious figure appeared in the light, and his ecstatic feelings reached a new zenith. The figure, he knew, and it knew him. The figure was light, the figure was power, the figure was love, the figure was joy.

This was Immanuel the King, the Son, the Word, the Messiah, the Alpha and Omega of all existence. This was I Am, this was Wonderful, this was the Counsellor, the mighty God, the everlasting Father, the Prince of Peace, the Redeemer.

Here stood the humble servant of the most lowly. Here stood the Savior of the world. Here stood the babe who was born in a manger. Here stood the mighty Lord, the Creator of worlds, the Jehovah of promise.

This was he who offered himself as a sacrifice for all who lived. This was he who was our mediator with the Father. This was he who was crucified for speaking the truth. This was he of whom the prophets had foretold and the angels had sung of for millennia. This was Jesus of Nazareth.

The glory emanating from this mighty being was beyond description. Everything about him glowed. His hair was a golden-brown color, and it extended to his collar. A neatly trimmed beard rimmed his full jaw, and brilliant blue eyes were set in a wide forehead. Under his glowing white robes, the muscular strength of his male figure was apparent. And above all were the feelings of love and knowledge that radiated from the reality of this magnificent personage.

The marvelous being smiled, and his desire to have Laura sit on a nearby rock was immediately transmitted. Brother Olvin, Brother Pratt and Brother Brigham moved close to the Savior and Laura, and they all placed their hands on Laura's head. A blessing was then pronounced on Laura, and she was set apart for her calling.

The Savior's words fell on Laura and the others present as the dew from heaven. She was blessed as a mother in Zion, as the mother of a prophet, and as one who would receive many of the same blessings bestowed by Abraham upon his posterity. She was given the gift of revelation as it related to the needs of her family and herself. Her good health and safety were assured through the time necessary to accomplish her mission. According to the faithfulness with which she fulfilled her calling, she was promised a full and joyful life, with the ability to reject Satan and his enticements. She was assured that she would have a full complement of those nurturing, teaching and loving talents essential to the proper development of her children—and for the fulfillment of the love between herself and her husband. Finally, she was promised that certain keys would be given her so that she would know her eternal companion when the time was right.

Elated over the blessing she'd just received, Laura wondered at the marvel of the moment. She never wanted it to end, but Brother Parley, Brother Brigham and Brother Olvin extended their love and withdrew.

The Savior remained with Laura and Mathias as they gazed at the magnificent valley beneath them, the enormous Valley of the Son. Pointing to the panorama of beauty stretching below them, the Son communicated the thought: *Drink of the beauty before you, and be filled with joy, for this stage of your progression is nearing completion. The next stage, Earth, will be even more marvelous if you magnify your callings.*

The Son then motioned to his side, and transmitted the thought: *Behold, the Earth.* There, for Laura and Mathias to view, as though suspended in space immediately to the side of the great valley, was a lovely blue planet.[2] Its presence was heralded by the aeolian strains of atmospheric melody. It was as if they were being welcomed by a new friend.

Transfixed by what they'd seen and heard, they gazed in wonder, marvelling at their feelings of ecstasy. The Son then smiled, the vision of Earth disappeared, and He transmitted the thought: *My blessings upon you both.* With that, the Son departed.

Sitting together in the large room, with several other persons present, Laura and Mathias were completing their pre-birth conferences. The time was near for them to depart for Earth.

Brother Brigham, Brother Parley and Brother Olvin were conducting the meeting. Other superior spirits were also present, apparently in the family lines of some of those awaiting Earthly experiences. Explaining some of the options available to those awaiting Earth-birth, Brother Brigham emphasized that the candidates for Earth were not obligated to choose any of the options, it was entirely their decision.

One lady had already indicated her choice of parents. She'd been given the option of choosing a poor, but honest family in China, or of selecting a much more wealthy but more materially oriented family in Spain. Each family offered certain developmental opportunities for the lady. She opted for the family in China.

A somewhat confused male spirit was uncertain about all of the options presented. Deciding to make none of the choices

---

2 This scene is depicted on the cover. The original oil, *Love's Eternal Legacy,* was painted by Florence Susan Comish of Provo, Utah, especially for this book.

himself, he left it up to the presiding spirits in the conference. He told them to choose for him, or to leave it to chance. Brother Brigham made some suggestions, and the individual accepted them.

Perhaps the most frightening choices presented to the group were those having to do with pain and illness. It was pointed out, for example, that a spirit could choose an Earth-life situation that invoked little pain or physical hardship. Growth, under these circumstances, would be less rapid than would be the case for someone who accepted a life of pain. In a somewhat analogous manner, those who accepted a life of poverty and difficult circumstances could, theoretically, advance more rapidly than a person who chose a life of ease. There were other mitigating factors, of course, and, it was explained that each case should involve a consideration of the unique needs of that case.

When it came time for Laura to make her choices, she chose, of course, the parents that had already been revealed to her—Alma and Janis Pratt. She also chose to go through life with a healthy body, so that she might properly perform the nurturing and protecting functions so important to her calling.

One aspect of Earth-life bothered Laura, the fact that she would forget everything about her previous life with Father and the Son. It was distressing to contemplate not being able to remember home. Brooding over that eventuality, after completing her choices, Laura said a silent, and earnestly felt prayer: *Father, please help me to remember this room when I go to Earth. Don't let me forget everything about home. Let me, in the future, catch a glimpse again of the beauty and wonder of this place—my home.*

Closing her prayer in the name of the Son, Laura examined the details of the room she was in, as if to ensure their retention in her memory. The high ceiling, with its delicate arches and chandeliers, the ornate wood carvings in the walls, the narrow windows with light streaming in, the sloping floor and cushioned chairs, the elevated stage and podium, the silver-threaded drapes covering the final door exit, all became a part of her prayed-for remembrance.

While Laura was struggling with her innermost thoughts, Mathias had finally decided on his choices. He transmitted those choices to Brother Olvin, Brother Brigham, Brother Pratt, and to

Laura. Laura heard her beloved's voice say: *I, of course, choose the family that I've been called to be a part of, Alvin and Sue Blair. Recognizing my weaknesses of pride, jealousy, and of my tendency for self-doubt and fear, however, I also choose to be afflicted throughout my life with an illness. It is a severe illness that will keep me humble and help me, though adversity, to grow so as to be a proper father of a prophet—and, with the Son's will, a loving husband to Laura. I choose, therefore, throughout my life on Earth to suffer with the disease known on Earth as cystic fibrosis.*

Struggling with her emotions, Laura next heard Brother Olvin say to Mathias: *That's a serious disability, Mathias, with significant pain. You've not experienced pain to this point in your existence. Do you understand what you're committing to?*

Yes, Brother Olvin, I do. I also understand my own weaknesses, and I need to put in place those challenges that will change my weaknesses to strengths. I think that these choices will help me accomplish my mission.

Are you sure?

Yes.

Are you sure?

Yes. I'm certain about my choices.

Are you sure?

Yes, and I'll love Laura forever.

Turning to embrace her beloved, Laura saw Mathias smile at her; then he was gone. Bound for Earth.

Laura looked again around the room that she wanted to remember. Brother Pratt smiled encouragement to her. Suddenly she felt herself being lifted into space. At first it was a familiar sensation—one that she'd experienced several times on her previous trips to Earth. Then . . . something happened. She no longer could remember where she was or what was happening. There was a warm, soothing sensation, and . . . and darkness. It was not a frightening darkness; in fact, there was a calming, nourishing feeling associated with the entire experience. Laura relaxed and surrendered herself to her surroundings.

Alvin Blair had completed his day at the General Electric nuclear facility where he worked as an administrative assistant. It had been a tiring day, and he looked forward to being with his wife and his two children. Tonight was Monday night, and the children would be looking forward to family night. It was Leah's turn to present the lesson, so Sue would undoubtedly be helping Leah to prepare it.

Sue had instructed Alvin to hurry home. She sounded a little anxious—that was probably just his imagination, though. He'd know soon enough.

Driving into his driveway, Alvin was surprised to see Sue waiting on the front step for him. She was smiling radiantly, and the two girls were sitting with her. As soon as he stepped from the car, Leah said: "Daddy, guess what? We're going to have a baby."

Alvin laughed, "Oh, *we* are, are we?" He was about to ask Sue if it were true, but looking at her face confirmed it.

She hastened to add, "The doctor said all the tests are positive. I'm about six weeks along. He'll arrive about next Christmas. What a wonderful Christmas present."

"That's true, Sue, but how do you know it's a boy?"

Smiling, Sue said, "Oh, I just know."

As they entered the house, Alvin paused and said: "Let me call Johnny and Barbara. I promised to notify them immediately if you became pregnant."

Barbara answered the phone. Alvin told her the news. "That's terrific, Alvin," she responded. "Sue must be ecstatic."

"She is, Barbara. The baby will arrive about Christmas."

"Let's see, that should be about a month after we have ours."

"What? You're pregnant, also?"

"Yes, I'm about two-and-a-half months along."

"How fantastic. Why didn't you call us?"

"We would have, shortly. I wanted to be sure that I was definitely pregnant. John is absolutely delighted."

"I'll bet he is. How's his health?"

"He continues to struggle. He jokes that he'll never be fat again, and that's probably true."

"Well, our love to you and John, Barbara. That's great news—we'll have to celebrate together."

Janis had arranged for a Saturday morning doctor's appointment while Alma worked on the corral with the boys. She could hardly wait to arrive home and tell him the news. He'd be pleased with part of the news, but she wasn't so sure how he'd take the rest. Her husband was a wonderful man, all that she ever wanted, but even though he was a bishop he didn't seem to have the faith that she did. Why was it, she wondered, that otherwise terrific men appeared to lean on their wives for faith?

Driving to the back yard where the boys were working on the corral, Janis stopped and got out. She laughed as she examined her tribe. "How can you three get so dirty over a few boards and fence posts?"

Chuckling, Alma kissed his wife. "What did the doctor have to say?"

Excitement filled Janis, yet she wondered how Alma would feel if he knew everything the doctor had told her. Should she tell him, or would it lead to needless worry on his part? . . .

"He confirmed that I'm pregnant, Alma. The baby will arrive, if all goes well, sometime in December."

What was Janis trying to tell him? Alma was thrilled, of course, but there were still risks. What had the doctor really said?

"If all goes well? Does that mean that there are complications?"

"You knew that he advised against our having another baby. He wants me to check in about twice as often as I did when we had Sherman."

"You carefully follow all of the doctor's advice, dear," Alma said with both excitement and concern in his voice. "We need our lovely wife and mother."

Chapter 16

BIRTHS, TRAUMAS AND BLESSINGS

The Angel that presided o'er my birth
Said, "Little creature, formed of joy and mirth,
*Go love without the help of any thing on earth." * [1]

Janis had returned from the doctor, and she was worried. She wondered how she would tell Alma. Everything had gone so well until now. The time left was only two months and it seemed that all her prayers had been answered; then she had noticed a little spotting of blood. She was sure it was just a temporary problem, but the doctor had been almost nasty as he chastised her. She was accustomed to his warnings, but when he threatened to put her in the hospital she knew that he was serious.

It was nearly time to prepare dinner and the two boys would be hungry, as would her husband—yet she was so tired. Probably she needed an insulin shot. Her blood sugar was a little high at the doctor's office. She'd give herself a shot, and then she'd do as the doctor recommended and just lie down for a few moments.

Janis was sure the insulin would restore her energy. Relaxing on the couch after her shot felt so good, that . . .

The ringing of the telephone jarred Janis awake. Stumbling to her feet she managed to reach the telephone and fall into a chair. Her foggy brain didn't seem to work right. Through the haze she

---

1 Blake, William, 1757-1827, *The Angel That Presided.* "Poems" (1807-1809) from Blake's Notebook.

159

recognized Lori's voice, but for some reason her tongue didn't want to work, and the words that came out weren't really words. Then everything went black.

🐛 🐛 🐛 🐛

When she became aware of her surroundings, Janis found herself in bed with wires attached to her and with a beeping electronic device near her bed. Holding her hand was Alma, and standing beside him was Lori.

"Thank the Lord, you're back. My darling, you really scared us that time," Alma said as he squeezed her hand. "What were you trying to do?"

"I was just so tired—I took an insulin shot and lay on the couch. Then . . ."

"That's what Doctor Lewis thought. Apparently you overdosed on the insulin and were going into shock when Lori called. Somebody must be watching out for you."

Smiling, Lori said, "It just seemed that I should be talking to you, Janis, so I phoned. Actually, I was about to go to the store, and the thought came that I should call you. I almost ignored it, figuring that we could talk later. Then I got an urgent feeling that I should call at once, so I did."

Sitting up in her bed, and looking at Alma, Janis asked, "Can I go home now? The kids need . . ."

Restraining her and looking serious, Alma said, "No. You can't go home now—not until after the baby has come. The kids are fine; they're with Lori's kids."

Tears filled Janis's eyes and she had a difficult time speaking. "But my boys . . . I can't stay here. What did you mean, Alma, I have to stay until after the baby comes? That's two months away."

"Doctor Lewis thinks it may be less, Janis, perhaps only four weeks. They may bring the baby early in order to protect your health."

"Even so, I can't stay here. I've got things I have to do right now. Four weeks is too . . ."

"Janis, you don't understand. If you keep going you could lose the baby—or your life."

"And Janis," interrupted Lori, "the boys can stay with us during the day, until Alma picks them up after work. You know they'll fit in with my kids. The Relief Society has agreed to help Alma with food and laundry."

Janis smiled weakly as she wiped away tears. "You guys have already figured it all out, haven't you?"

Alma bent down and kissed his wife. "It's because we love you, dearest—and we need you. We want you to be well and strong."

Janis stayed in Castle View Hospital for a week-and-a-half. Her system had improved enough by then for the doctor to release her—subject to her promise that she'd not overdo.

For almost three weeks Janis did reasonably well. Then, one evening, as she and the boys were watching television, she said to her oldest boy: "Jeremy, call Dad at the bishop's office and tell him I think the time is now. Have him hurry home."

🌱   🌱   🌱   🌱

Alma arrived home ten minutes later and rushed Janis to the hospital. Doctor Lewis had already arrived and was waiting for them. "Well, Janis. It looks as if you're going to have a Thanksgiving present."

"Doctor, I'm so excited about this baby. We can hardly wait for her to come."

Janis was prepped, and she waited in her room with Alma while the nurse kept checking her. Finally, the time came and she was wheeled into the delivery room. Alma stayed with her and encouraged her during the birth contractions.

Through her pain Janis heard Doctor Lewis say: "That's it, Janis. Push hard. I can see the head—it's just a little more now."

Janis heard the doctor say, "That's it, here she comes, she's a beautiful baby girl." Almost simultaneously the nurse shouted, "Doctor, Janis is hemorrhaging!"

"I see," he said, "Nurse, put the blood clotting medication into her IV, quick. If that doesn't work we'll have to get her to OR for an emergency operation. Alert them. And Alma, get out."

Janis felt intense pain, and then, nothing—

Suddenly Janis was standing next to the bed watching the doctor and nurses frantically work on her. The scene was so strange that at first she didn't understand what was happening. She had the thought: *How can I be up here with the doctor working on me down there?*

Just as this thought hit, she saw what appeared to be a dark hole, or a tunnel, with light streaming from it. She moved toward the light, and as she did she felt enormous peace—in fact, the light seemed to have a personality with tremendous love coming from it.

Her pain had completely vanished, and she drifted toward that wonderful light—that beautiful bright white light. She was overwhelmed and wanted with everything in her to move into the light. Then, in her mind, she heard a man's voice say: *It's not your time, you must go back. You have a husband to take care of and children to raise. You have a new baby—a daughter.*

Then the thought came to her: *I've got a new baby girl, the marvelous girl I saw that night. I've got to go back.*

The next thing Janis knew she was awake, in the hospital bed, and she felt hungry. Alma was sitting alongside the bed looking concerned.

Smiling weakly, Janis said, "I'm hungry."

"Wonderful," said Alma. "Let me call the nurse. You slept for twenty-four hours."

"At least for part of the time I wasn't asleep. I was in another place, it was . . . I was out of my body. The doctor and nurses were working on me, and I saw them from up near the ceiling. Then a voice told me to come back."

"Doctor Lewis said they lost you for a while. It's a good thing we gave you a blessing before you went into delivery."

"How's the baby? Did she . . . ?"

"She's fine. She has red hair."

Remembering the gorgeous girl with the red hair that she had seen in vision that night, Janis started to cry. Wiping her tears, she said, "I knew she'd have red hair. May I see her?"

"Of course. But let's get some food in you first."

"Alma—."

"What?"

"What would you think if we called her Laurel?"

"Laurel? That's an interesting name. How did you come up with that?"

"I don't know. It just seems like the right name."

"Sure, we can call her Laurel, if that's what you want."

John Blair, Jr. arrived right on schedule in late November, shortly after Janis and Alma had Laurel. Considering that it was Barbara's first, and that she had recently had her fortieth birthday, the baby's birth was relatively uneventful—except to the parents. Both professors were elated.

After the birth, John proudly called his brother Alvin and asked him to bless the baby during their December Fast Meeting. Alvin agreed, and Sue—a very pregnant Sue—and the two girls all witnessed the blessing.

Barbara took notes as the blessing proceeded, and she thrilled when she heard Alvin say, ". . . and you will grow to manhood as a highly intelligent person; you'll be active in your church, and you'll be a constant joy to your parents. . . ." Barbara squeezed John's hand as the blessing continued.

After the Church service, Alvin asked his brother, "Has your Bishop said anything yet, Johnny, about when you might get the Melchizedek Priesthood and go to the temple?"

"He said the Stake President thinks that this might happen in the next two or three months."

"Mom will be overjoyed," said Alvin.

"I know. When I think of how I hurt her by leaving the Church—"

"That will all be changed when you go through the temple, Johnny. What a day that'll be."

Sue was lying in the hospital bed of Good Samaritan Hospital in San Jose. The delivery had not been difficult—the baby had been small—but he seemed normal, and the doctor didn't say anything. *So, where was Alvin, and why couldn't she see her baby? Why didn't somebody tell her what was going on?*

Being tired from the delivery, Sue would have slept, but she continued to fret about the baby. *Where was Alvin, anyhow? How could he be so thoughtless as to leave her to wonder about the baby?*

As she worried about the baby Sue said a silent prayer: *Please, Father, take my fears away. Let everything be okay for the little fellow. Help us to be good parents, and bless him so that he'll grow and develop . . .*

Closing her prayer, Sue watched as Alvin walked into the room, followed by Dr. Nelson, the pediatrician. She was alarmed at the serious looks on their faces. She was almost afraid to ask, "What is it Alvin? Is there something wrong with . . . ?"

Alvin sat next to her, reached for her hand, and looked at the doctor. "There appears to be some difficulty, Sue," the doctor began. "The baby had problems breathing."

Beginning to cry, Sue tried to control her emotions, but with not much success. "But Doctor, he seemed normal at birth, just a little small. The poor little fellow, what can we . . . ?" Sue lapsed into tears as a feeling of helplessness hit her. She continued with difficulty. "What's causing the breathing problems?"

"We aren't sure, we're running several tests, but until we get the results we won't know."

Over the next several days, Sue was released from the hospital, but despite Alvin's and Sue's prayers, and the efforts of the doctors, the baby seemed to languish. After several tests had been run the doctor called them to meet with him.

The receptionist ushered Alvin and Sue into Dr. Nelson's office. Sue had hardly been seated when she began asking questions. "Do you know what's the matter with Michael, Doctor? Do you know what's wrong?"

"We're not certain, but we think so. I've consulted with some specialists and they agree with my tentative diagnosis. It appears that your child has cystic fibrosis."

Sue began to cry. Alvin swallowed deeply as he tried to remain calm. "What's cystic fibrosis, and how does it work?"

"It's a genetic disease, produced when the child inherits dominant genes from both parents. The disease is characterized by problems in the pulmonary system, the lungs, and in the digestive tract."

"What can we do?" Sue asked.

"There currently is no cure, although much can be done to reduce the bad effects of the disease."

"Will we be able to take him home?" Sue asked.

"If his system stabilizes in the next week or so, then you may take him home."

Alvin was pensive as he listened to the doctor. "What's the life expectancy of cystic fibrosis patients, doctor?"

"In severe pulmonary cases the prognosis is not very good—maybe into their twenties. If the disease is kept under control, and if it's not too severe, then the patient can enjoy a reasonably good lifetime into their forties, fifties or even longer. It's a serious disease, though, and should be treated accordingly."

After leaving the doctor's office, Sue sat reading a pamphlet as Alvin drove the car. Suddenly she said, "We need to do one other thing that the doctor didn't mention."

"What's that, Sue?"

"You need to give him a blessing."

The drive to the hospital was made in relative silence. All of them, including their normally talkative home teacher, Brother Hodgson, were occupied with their own thoughts and prayers. Arriving at the hospital, the nurses equipped them with green hospital gowns and masks before they allowed them to enter the nursery where critical-care babies were kept. They were cautioned about staying too long.

Sue gasped when she saw Michael. "Oh, you poor little thing. Alvin, he looks worse than he did yesterday. Look how he struggles to get air. The diaper seems too large for him. If he loses any more weight there'll be nothing . . ."

Alvin and Brother Hodgson moved close to the baby while Sue stood in the background with her note pad. Brother Hodgson produced a drop of oil from his vial and quickly anointed the baby. Then both men gently placed their fingers on the baby and Alvin began the blessing. Sue listened carefully so that she could accurately record what was said. The blessing seemed to proceed in a normal fashion until Alvin, for no apparent reason, stopped. Sue looked at him in surprise—he appeared to be struggling with himself. Then she heard these electric words:

". . . Michael, you've been chosen for a unique mission, and you'll live to fulfill that mission. Your health will be adequate for you to meet all the commitments that you made prior to this life. By the power of the Melchizedek Priesthood, which we hold, we bless you so that from this point on your lungs will be strengthened and your breathing will be improved. We further bless your parents so that they will know, together with the doctors, what to do for your proper care.

"We say to you, Michael, that you will grow to adulthood and be a joy to your parents. As a young man, you'll serve a mission for your Lord and Savior, and you'll ultimately be sealed to an eternal companion—and you'll have children. You'll be able to meet those challenges which . . ."

There were several other promises, recorded with difficulty by Sue as she sought to comprehend what she had just heard Alvin say. She could hardly wait to question him about it.

Brother Hodgson was the first to break the silence as they drove home. Amazed at what he'd heard, he said, "That was quite a blessing you gave your son, Brother Blair."

"Yes, Alvin. I thought so too," said Sue. "You said that he was chosen for a unique mission. What did you mean by that?"

"I don't know what it meant. The blessing was proceeding as they normally do, and I felt . . . how can I explain it? All of sudden, it was as though words came into my mind. It was the strangest sensation—it seemed, almost, that I was a bystander in the blessing."

"You also promised that he'd grow to adulthood, serve a mission, and have children. Do you remember?"

"How could I forget? Let's hope it was the Spirit speaking through me, and not just my own desire."

Over the next week Alvin and Sue visited the baby each day. To Sue's eyes he seemed to be improving, but she wasn't sure whether it was real or just her strong desire.

Alvin, too, thought he saw improvement, but he was afraid to say anything to Sue. Not wanting to build her hopes too high, and then have them dashed, he kept quiet. Then, a little over a week after the blessing, Sue called him at work. She was crying.

"Alvin, Dr. Nelson called, he . . ." she was unable to continue.

"It's okay, Sue. Take your time. Is the baby worse?"

"No. He's better," and now Sue was laughing and crying at the same time.

"What do you mean he's better? He still has cystic fibrosis doesn't he?"

"Yes. In fact they got the DNA test back and it confirmed cystic fibrosis."

"Well then . . . ?"

"I'm trying to tell you. Dr. Nelson said that starting about a week ago Michael's vital signs began to improve—all of them. His lungs cleared up and he's breathing almost normally. Alvin, he's gained a half-pound in this last week. The doctor says that we can take him home next week if he continues to improve."

🍒   🍒   🍒   🍒

Michael Blair came home one week later. Leah immediately asked, "Mama, can we show him to our friends?"

"Not at first, dear. Remember what the doctor said about protecting him against colds. In fact, when you girls get the sniffles you'll have to stay away from him."

Looking at her priceless bundle, Sue said a silent prayer of thanks. Her prayer included a promise to do all in her power to help him grow to maturity. Looking at her husband and children, she had a surge of overwhelming love. Life was good.

Chapter 17

A TEMPLE EXPERIENCE

Holy temples on Mount Zion in a lofty splendor shine,
Avenues to exaltation, Symbols of a love divine.
And their kindly portals beckon to serenity and prayer,
Valiant children of the promise, Pledged to sacred service there.[1]

It was early summer, and the California hills were turning their usual golden-brown. Barbara was thoroughly enjoying her role as wife and mother, and she frequently took John, Jr. on rides in the country. Resigning her position as a tenured professor of law at the University of California had taken courage, but John had encouraged it. She still taught an occasional class and she did some consulting, but her primary interest now was John, Jr.

This afternoon she was driving to San Jose to visit with Sue. Later in the day John would join them after he completed his class schedule. She continued to be amazed at John's changed character. Laughing to herself as she thought about the paper John was writing for a conference on philosophy to be held in Carmel in a few months, she strained to remember the title. Chuckling again, she remembered: *The Development of the Philosophic Milieu in Western Civilization at the Exclusion of the Religious Experience—Some Examples.*

---

1 Bennett, Archibald F., 1896-1965, *Hymns of The Church of Jesus Christ of Latter-day Saints,* Published by The Church of Jesus Christ of Latter-day Saints, Salt Lake City, Utah, 1985, p. 289.

169

There was no doubt in Barbara's mind that the paper would be well received by John's colleagues; his papers always were. Even though this paper represented a complete repudiation of everything John had previously written about, it would attract many in the academic community for just that reason. Many wondered what had gotten into John.

At times Barbara wondered herself. Not that she didn't enjoy their new spirituality; it was a thrill when Alvin baptized her and rebaptized John. The meeting with a General Authority was set for next week, and both she and John could hardly wait. No, she would never wish to return to their previous lifestyle. It was just that sometimes . . . *why did John have to be so intense about it? What difference did it make if she watched television, or wanted to go to a movie now and then. After all, she read her scriptures, just not all day. John had become almost fanatic on the subject.*

Barbara sighed as she thought about her husband. John, Jr. whimpering in his baby carrier interrupted her thoughts. "Patience, Junior. We're almost there, and then you can have your bottle. Maybe we can give you a bath at Aunt Sue's house."

Pulling in to Sue's driveway in the Almaden area of San Jose, Barbara saw Sue look out the window. What a wonderful person Sue was, and how happy Barbara was that they'd become such friends. And to think that she previously thought of Alvin and Sue as uncultured and undereducated. In the things that mattered most she and John had learned immensely from their brother- and sister-in-law.

Carrying all of Junior's "life-support systems" into Sue's house would be a problem if it weren't for Sue's help. Barbara grunted as she struggled to get the play pen out the back door.

"You remind me of myself when we had our first one," Sue laughed. "We used to have bottle warmers, special formula, clean diapers, diaper wipes, blankets, toys, pillows, pacifiers, and assorted emergency equipment. Then when Rose came we gave up most of it. Now with Michael, we've had to go back to taking everything with us—when we travel at all, that is."

"How's Michael doing?" Barbara asked.

"See for yourself. He's struggling to sit up, already. He's not as athletic as Junior, of course," she laughed, "but we no longer feel that we're in danger of losing him."

"I'm so happy for you, Sue."

Chatting happily about their babies, Sue and Barbara didn't notice the rapid passage of time until the door banged and John came in. Smiling broadly, he kissed his wife and hugged Sue. Then he laughed.

"What is it John?" Barbara asked.

"The Stake President called before I left my office. He confirmed our date with the General Authority next Tuesday."

"But you knew that already. Why are you laughing?"

"It's just . . . I never thought I'd see that day again. When I left the Church I thought it was forever. Not that I wanted to come back, but now . . . everything's different."

"You're not kidding, everything's different. The man I married died, and a different man returned in his place. Sometimes I wonder which one I prefer." The both laughed at their private joke.

❥   ❥   ❥   ❥

It was dark on Friday morning when Alvin and Sue arrived with Mother Blair. Entering John's and Barbara's spacious Berkeley home high on Spruce Street, Sue still was impressed with the view. The bay area lights spilled from the surrounding hills onto the bay in a shimmering celebration of the day. The first streaks of dawn from the east did their best to illuminate the early morning fog bank pressing, like a marching army, through the Golden Gate.

John greeted them in the entrance hall. "Thanks for coming. I know it's an awful hour, but they told us to be at the temple by 5:30 a.m. Why so early, I have no idea. I hardly slept last night, though, so I might as well be in the temple."

Alvin could see that John seemed a little nervous. "Today will be a marvelous day, John, but don't expect to remember everything that you see from this first visit. The beauty of the temple ceremony is that you can attend many times in the future, to do vicarious work for the dead, and in the process learn more of what the temple service means. It's a spiritual feast."

The temple service was more complicated and took longer than John had anticipated. Alvin was right, thought Johnny, as he struggled to understand everything he'd heard and seen. It was too much to absorb in one sitting—even for a professor—and John smiled as he thought of some of his erudite colleagues and their opinions of religious liturgies. John knew that he wouldn't have accepted it so well, himself, had it not been for the near-death experience he'd undergone.

At one point in the ceremony, while he was attempting to fathom the deepest meaning from what he saw and heard, he looked around the room with the people all dressed in white, and he saw . . . it was astonishing. He saw the same scene that he had previously seen in vision during his NDE. When he originally saw this scene, shortly after having seen a vision of the temple building with its towers, it was in the context of something that would happen in his future—if he chose to return to life. And how grateful he was that he chose to return. What he would have missed if he hadn't come back!

Finally, with his head and heart full to overflowing, the endowment was completed and they all met in what was called the celestial room. The beauty of the room added an ethereal charm to the setting, and John and Barbara sat holding hands. So as not to disturb the feeling of reverence they all enjoyed, Alvin slipped out and called his mother, asking her to bring Junior.

After a period of restful meditation, Alvin led them to another room. It was smaller than the rooms they previously had been in, and it had mirrors on two walls with a padded altar in the middle of the room. An officiator sat behind a table at the head of the room, and relatives and friends congregated on a padded bench arranged around the sides of the room.

Wearing a gigantic smile, Martha Blair entered the room. Sitting next to Barbara and Sue, she whispered an explanation when Barbara looked puzzled because John, Jr. was not with her.

"Junior is with one of the temple workers, Barbara. He'll be brought in a little later."

Relaxing somewhat from the surprise of not having seen her son with her mother-in-law, Barbara forced her mind to concentrate on what the priesthood officiator was saying to them. He was asking John and her to kneel across from each other at the altar.

As they knelt looking at each other, Barbara felt enormous love for this wonderful man who had brought her to this point in her life. Then she listened to the words being spoken by the officiator. They were words of tremendous promise, words that bound her together with her husband for an eternity. Concentrating on the words so that she'd remember them later, Barbara glanced again at John and was astonished to see tears tumbling from his eyes. When she smiled at her husband in an attempt to gently reassure him, he smiled back, but the tears continued to flow.

Upon completion of the sealing ceremony, John and Barbara kissed, and a temple matron brought John, Jr. into the room. On this occasion it was Barbara's turn to cry as her precious son was sealed to her and John for all time and eternity. Feeling, again, a surging sense of love and peace, Barbara basked in the beauty and serenity of the entire scene. She felt that she could stay there forever.

Later, after congratulations had been offered by the many friends who were present, the family drove home and assembled in John's large living room. A servant brought them light refreshments and took Junior to his playpen.

They conversed for some time about the remarkable things they'd seen and heard, but Barbara was concerned because John kept crying. The others in the room tried not to notice, but finally Barbara asked, "What is it John? Is something the matter?"

Looking at the others in the room, John said, with difficulty, "Didn't any of you see them?"

"See who, Johnny?" Alvin asked.

"Dad and Jim—and somebody else. They were sitting next to Mom on the bench. Didn't you see them, Mom?"

Martha was crying, now. "No, Johnny, I didn't see them, but I thought I felt a presence."

"Did they say or do anything?" Alvin asked.

"No. They smiled at me, and they just sat next to Mom while Barbara and I were sealed. Then they left."

"Remarkable," Barbara said as she wiped her eyes. "Does this sort of thing happen often?"

"Probably more often than many people think," Sue remarked. "But, no. It's not a frequent occurrence. From those who've shared such experiences with me, it seems to be in response to a special need."

"You said that there was someone else besides Dad and Jim, Johnny. Do you know who that was?" Alvin asked.

"No, but . . . I could feel love coming from him, and . . ."

"What, Johnny?"

"I don't know. He seemed important, somehow."

Approaching dusk cast its magic spell over thc bay as shimmering lights again twinkled a greeting at the enthralled travelers returning home from their thrilling day. Riding along in silence for awhile, Martha broke the silence by asking, almost to herself, the question: "Why couldn't I see Olvin or Jim?"

"Because, Mom, I think Sue was right. They showed themselves to Johnny who had a greater need than any of us. Look what his near-death experience has done for him."

"Yes, Mother Blair," Sue continued. "Johnny has some catching up to do, and this will help him. It'll also help others whom he feels impressed to tell of his experience."

"It certainly will," Mother Blair said solemnly. "When Olvin died, and later, Jim, I wondered why I was being singled out for such tragedies. Now, although I don't completely understand the reasons for their being taken, I see it as part of their continuing missions."

Standing in the location that he knew to be his mother-select's favorite location, Barnabas was exhilarated with all that had happened in the most recent revolutions of Kolob-1. He had been privileged to visit Earth with Brother Olvin and Brother Jim, his relatives-select. The temple ceremony, in which he had witnessed the bestowal of celestial blessings on his future relatives, was thrilling.

And now, his mother-select! The only mother he'd ever known was Mother. Would Laura be as nurturing, supportive and wise as Mother? After all, when he had doubts about his future calling as a prophet for Father, it was Mother that encouraged him. It was She who had reminded him of his valiancy in the great war, when the uncertainties and risks were much greater than his calling on Earth would be.

Elapsed time before his birth-life, he understood, would be but the blink of an eye. Earth time would pass slowly for those awaiting his arrival, but not here. He still found the Earthly concept of time to be a curious one—and the idea of measuring it seemed preposterous. Teacher Gallexus and Brother Pratt had both assured him that time, and other difficult Earthly notions, would be more familiar to him when his birth-life arrived. From now until his birth Barnabas must devote his energy and attention to the accelerated preparation program that Brother Pratt and Brother Brigham had arranged for him.

Devoting much of his recent Quiets to prayer on behalf of his mother- and father-selects, he vowed to intensify such prayers. The uncertainty in his father-select's calling was unnerving to them all. Mathias's choice of a disabling disease during his Earth life was reassuring in a way. It showed Mathias's commitment to following through with his calling as father-select to a prophet.

With all the risks involved in Earth life, Barnabas wondered how his life would work out. Having viewed many futures of various possible events of his Earth life, he had a fair idea of what might happen. Those futures, though, were filled with imponderables that could alter the outcome significantly. Agency, as provided in The Plan, was marvelous in guaranteeing growth potential for humans, but that very guarantee also made much of the future unpredictable—at least for most humble spirits such as himself.

Assuming that he'd grow to fill the measure of his calling, the future might be less uncertain. But for now, questions continued to persist about what might happen. *Would Mathias be able to cope with the illness, cystic fibrosis? Would Laura and Mathias find themselves on Earth, and would they recognize each other and become husband and wife if they did find themselves? Would war, civil disturbance, natural cataclysm, political instability, economic disaster, or other distress, which could, and often did intrude on Earthly affairs, disrupt the carefully laid plans associated with his calling? If such disturbances occurred, could his parents-select respond in time to remedy the damage? Could Satan disrupt the whole plan? Could . . .?*

Deciding to end his Quiet in a heartfelt prayer, Barnabas began:

Father, thou who knowest all, bless me. Please calm my troubled spirit. Help me to grow in faith, in knowledge, in wisdom, and in courage to face the uncertainties of the future.

And Father, please bless those who will become a part of my future. Bless Janis Pratt that she might have the strength to nurture Laura, and bless Laura that she might have all the facilities that she will need to grow and develop properly. Please, Father, look down upon Mathias. Help Alvin and Sue Blair to be able to obtain proper medical care for Mathias. Help him to have the strength to grow to maturity, and help him to live up to his full potential.

Arrange conditions on Earth, Father, so that they'll be conducive for the meeting and growth of the love of Mathias and Laura for each other. Let them recognize each other—or at least, feel a familiarity that will later grow into love.

Please provide angels for my family-select and for me during our Earthly sojourn. Give us the prescience to be sensitive to the prompting of the Spirit and to recognize and listen to angels which thou hast sent.

Above all, Father, bless me that I might never lose the knowledge of thee and thy Son. Strengthen my faith so that I might always be able to communicate with thee, and so that I will have the necessary knowledge and power to carry out my mission. Give me a continuing sense of that mission.

Finally, help me to have the peace and love that I feel here and now. Let me retain that gift on Earth, that I might use it for the benefit of others as well as myself.

I thank thee, Father, for my many blessings. I thank thee for life itself, and for The Plan which thou introduced before the great war. I thank thee for the enormous gift of thy Son, and help me to forever remember him. Thy faith in me is understood, and I will do my utmost to respond to that faith by devoting my entire being to the needs of my calling—I thank thee, I thank thee, I thank thee. . . .

Completing his prayer in the name of the Son, Barnabas let his spirit soar to one of the natural satellites that continually orbited Kolob-1. From space, he circled the satellite and observed the splendor of the beautiful planet that was his home.

Gazing at the ethereal essence of Kolob-1, with the brightly shining stars from the nearby Elohim Galaxy, Barnabas was filled with the Light. Feelings of peace, happiness, wonder, love, ecstasy, and power flowed into him with an amazing energy. Soaring through space and trailing streams of glory, he became, for a moment, a primary source of life, of joy, of creation. He knew, in that instant, that he was viewing his future. It was a limitless future, bounded only by the creativity and imagination that would be his in an infinity of growth.

Surrendering to the glory that engulfed him, and in an exuberance of joy, Barnabas sped to Kolob-Star and orbited that mighty energy source—a source created and energized by the Father and the Son. His understanding of the creative process was sharpened as he drank from the source of all knowledge. It was a source that satiated his being with feelings of eternal bliss, and it was a source that endowed him with promises that extended into infinity.

A sense within him let him know that this was all he would be allowed to view. Enjoying perfect understanding, he headed home—home to the fair planet Kolob-1. Enormous gratitude filled his spirit.   Adding a postscript to his earlier prayer, Barnabas expressed himself with difficulty.   He began and ended with the same thought.   It was a thought that he never would lose.

Father, I thank thee, I thank thee, I thank thee, I thank thee, I thank thee, I thank thee . . .

Chapter 18

DÉJÀ VU

❦   ❦   Two Earth Decades Later   ❦   ❦

But often, in the world's most crowded streets,
But often, in the din of strife,
There rises an unspeakable desire
After the knowledge of our buried life;
A thirst to spend our fire and restless force
In tracking out our true, original course;
A longing to inquire
Into the mystery of this heart which beats
So wild, so deep in us—to know
Whence our lives come and where they go.[1]

It was spring quarter, and Michael had recently celebrated his twenty-second birthday. After returning from his Arizona mission Michael spent a short time with his parents in San Jose, California, and then he returned to Brigham Young University. Currently, he was living with his sister, Leah, in Provo. Leah was married to an Associate Professor of English, Cody Keddington, who taught at the University. His sister and brother-in-law were kind enough to invite him to stay with them during the school year.

Michael was grateful for the help Leah and Cody offered him. Having helped her mother raise Michael, Leah was completely familiar with his cystic fibrosis and with emergency measures to be

---

1 Arnold, Mathew, 1822-1888, *The Buried Life*, 1852, l. 45-55.

taken when he got a bowel blockage, or when mucous in his chest couldn't be readily discharged.

Hating the fact that he frequently had difficult medical problems, Michael quickly accepted the offer by Leah and Cody to live with them. The idea of introducing someone else to his medical problems was not attractive. That was one of the hardest things about his mission in Arizona—to instruct a new companion what to do in the event of an emergency. Fortunately, the mission president was sympathetic to his problems and provided substantial help, particularly when Michael was moved into the mission home to assist with the financial records.

Changing from social science to mechanical engineering at the University had been traumatic at first, but he was glad that he'd made the switch. It was that trip through the Hunter Power Plant just before his mission that had persuaded him he should be involved in an engineering career.

Seeking ways to help Michael through his many medical crises, some years back, Sue and Alvin Blair had sent him to spend a summer with Sue's sister, Lori, in the Price region of Utah. At the time, Sue said that she had a strong impression that Michael should go to Utah. It had been a wonderful experience for Michael, living with his four cousins, and his health improved sufficiently to convince everyone that he could serve a mission.

During that wonderful summer Michael met Brother Alma Pratt and his wife Janis—close friends of his Aunt Lori. Brother Pratt took an interest in Michael and invited him to tour the Hunter Plant where Brother Pratt was the manager. It was a thrilling experience, and it affected Michael sufficiently that he decided to change his major when he returned from his mission.

Remembering back to that enchanted summer, Michael knew that the biggest thrill had been meeting the daughter of Alma and Janis Pratt. Laurel Pratt, who was the same age as Michael, was a breath of springtime. Her long red hair, and her sparkling blue eyes—which were perpetually laughing—attracted all within sight.

His older cousins, Alice and Ruth, treated Laurel as a younger sister, and she frequently spent time at Aunt Lori's house. She appeared to enjoy the horses that the Blairs kept. She was always friendly to Michael, and she spent much time with him—even though he wondered what Laurel saw in him. He was two inches shorter than she was, and it was obvious that she was popular with many of the local boys.

Despite Michael's feelings of inferiority, he and Laurel became close friends during the summer. Sharing many personal thoughts and goals, they spent long hours discussing the future. Laurel had boundless enthusiasm for all of life and seemed completely entranced by each day's opportunities. Michael, because of his illness, frequently approached a new day with dread. Laurel helped him to understand that even difficult periods could provide new chances for growth of the spirit, if not the body.

Laurel, in fact, became the focus for Michael of that fabulous summer. She seemed interested in his every thought and was sympathetic to his ideas of the future.

Wondering about Laurel's feelings for him during that summer, Michael sometimes dreamt the impossible dream. It was a dream of an unlimited future—a future that involved him and Laurel. It was a future which spoke of love, and family, and growth, and . . . In a way the dream seemed to encompass a distant part of him, a part that reached into his very soul and created an intense longing. A longing . . . for what?. . . He quickly put such thoughts out of his mind. There was no point in agonizing over what could never be.

When Michael left on his mission Laurel promised to write him regularly. In the beginning the letters came two or three times a week. Gradually, they became less frequent, perhaps once every week or every other week. Then came the fateful day, near the end of his mission, when he received the letter that began: "Dear Michael—I have met the most wonderful young man. . . ." He still winced as he thought back to that day. For a time it even affected his performance on his mission.

Returning to BYU had been a delightful experience, and Michael launched into his studies with vigor. Due to the need to concentrate on the subjects that led to an engineering degree, he had no social relationships for the first few weeks, aside from attending church. Inwardly he knew that he was avoiding social contact because of his fears.

There was the fear of embarrassment associated with explaining his illness—that was always traumatic. Then there was the fear that he would be rejected by someone he might like. The biggest fear, though, was the fear of approaching Laurel. Desiring with all his heart to meet her again, yet terrified of the prospect, he used his studies as an excuse for delaying the inevitable.

Knowing that Laurel was taking a full course of social studies, leading toward a degree in psychology, Michael walked to that part of the BYU campus in the off-chance that he might see her. No such luck—and he almost sighed with relief.

Finally, one day after a night of fitful anxiety, he gathered his courage and called her. When she came on the line, he greeted her with a trembling voice: "Hi Laurel, this is Michael," thinking to himself, *what a stupid way to begin.*

"Michael, how wonderful. Mom told me that you'd returned from your mission, and I was hoping you'd call. Where are you?"

"I'm staying with my sister here in Provo while I attend the Y."

"That's terrific. Why don't we get together soon? I'd like you to meet my fiancé."

"Your fiancé?"

"Yes. I wrote and told you about the wonderful young man that I met—Cal Simonds."

"I remember. I didn't know that you were engaged, though."

"I'm sorry. That's what happens when you get too involved. I should have told you. Anyhow, when can we meet?"

"Well, I'm not sure. I've switched majors, to engineering, and there's lots of catching up to do. . . ."

"Oh come on, Michael. Surely you can spare an hour to get together for old time's sake—and to meet Cal. How about tomorrow at 11:00 at the Wilkinson Center?"

"I've got a class at 11:00."

"Okay, then you tell me when."

"Well let's see. I guess I'm clear at noon."

"Great. We'll see you then in the cafeteria."

Spending another fitful night with little sleep, Michael had a difficult time concentrating in his morning classes. When his eleven o'clock class let out he almost considered cancelling the meeting with Laurel, but he didn't know how to get in touch with her. Walking slowly to the Wilkinson Center, he glanced around the cafeteria, half hoping that they wouldn't be there. There was no missing that flash of red hair though, and the delighted laugh that came from Laurel when she saw him.

Waving at him, Laurel shouted: "Michael, over here."

Many in the room glanced at Michael to see who was the focus of attention of the beautiful redhead. Trying to be inconspicuous, Michael nervously walked to Laurel's table.

Jumping from her chair, Laurel threw her arms around Michael and laughed the enchanting laugh he remembered from that wonderful summer—the laugh that had burned into his memory. Then he noticed . . . an enormous dark-haired young man standing next to Laurel and smiling at him. He was a full head taller than Michael, and his shoulders were . . ."

"Michael, this is Cal, my fiancé. And Cal, this is the fellow I told you about."

"Michael, I'm glad to meet you. Laurel has told me so much about you."

"Thanks. Laurel wrote about you, but you're so big. . . ." Michael was immediately sorry that he said what he did when both Laurel and Cal laughed. *Why was he socially so inept? His sisters had tried to teach him, but Michael always seemed to say and do the wrong thing in social situations. What a lousy beginning with Laurel!*

"Cal's a tight end on the football team, and that accounts for part of his size," Laurel laughed. "His parents also are tall, though, so he comes by it naturally."

"Sit down and join us, Michael," Cal said. "Why don't you pick up something at the cafeteria counter, and we can eat lunch."

"No thanks. I'm not hungry right now. I'll join you for a few minutes, then I've got to go."

There were a few moments of awkward silence at the table as Michael sat down. Then he asked: "When are you getting married?"

"It's scheduled for early August, before football practice starts," responded Cal.

"Cal is taking computer science," Laurel said, "and between his studies and football we have a hard time seeing each other." Laurel and Cal laughed.

"I see." Michael said.

"How was your mission, Michael?" Laurel asked.

"It was terrific," Michael said, finally feeling that he could communicate on a subject he felt confident about. "My mission president was a wonderful person, and I fell in love with the people in Arizona."

"Missions are great," Cal remarked.

"Did you serve a mission?" Michael asked.

"Yes," Cal said.

"Cal was one of the first missionaries to go into Hungary," Laurel enthusiastically commented.

"That must have been a real challenge," Michael said. Was the language difficult?"

"It was at first. Later, I got so that I was pretty good at it. At least that's what the mission president said."

Another silence ensued, followed by Michael saying: "Well, it was good seeing you both. I should go."

"Not so fast, Michael," Laurel said. "When can we get together so I can find out about your mission?"

"I'm not sure. Besides, you're busy with Cal, and . . ."

"Cal won't mind if we get together, will you Cal?"

Cal looked at Michael, as if sizing him up. Then he smiled a broad smile and said: "Of course not." Looking at Laurel and winking, he said: "You two need to talk over old times and Michael's mission."

Smiling back at Cal, Laurel directed her gaze at Michael. "How about tomorrow night, say nine o'clock? We could meet here again at the Wilkinson Center—okay?"

"Yes. That's okay."

Spending another restless night, Michael wondered if he would be able to keep up his grades. He struggled to stay awake in an afternoon class on differential equations, and he worried later about how he would catch up. Finally, the evening came and he walked to the Wilkinson Center. Laurel was waiting.

"Hi Michael. Shall we stay here, or would you like to go somewhere?"

"I don't have a car, Laurel."

"I've borrowed Cal's car, Michael, and we can use that if you'd like. Where would you like to go?"

"It doesn't matter. Wherever you'd like."

"Have you ever been to Rock Canyon, up Provo Canyon? You can drive up high and get a beautiful view of the stars away from all the lights."

"That sounds nice."

Driving in silence, they immersed themselves in their private thoughts. Michael wondered how many times Laurel had driven up Rock Canyon with some other fellow. Laurel broke into his thoughts by saying: "I thought of you often on your mission, but toward the end things got sort of hectic with Cal and everything."

"I understand."

Pulling onto a plateau high above the valley, Laurel parked the car and let the convertible top down. The night had deepened and a sliver of a moon rose in the eastern sky; Venus followed as though obeying some immutable law. Wisps of clouds passing over the moon's face gave it a sublime look. Overhead, Orion and the Big Dipper blinked their eternal messages. The sky was enormous and the stars were bright beyond belief. The Milky Way stretched in an endless band across empty space—a ballet of light pirouetting in the velvet night. Laurel broke their reverie.

"What are you thinking, Michael?"

Startled, Michael thought to himself: *If I could only tell her how much I love her. If I could put my arms around her and promise to be hers forever. . . .*

Instead, he said, "I was just looking at the stars."

"Aren't they beautiful? On a night like this, when I look at the stars, it seems as though . . ."

Michael was surprised to hear Laurel's voice break. She was wiping tears from her eyes. "What is it?" he asked.

"It's as though I am reliving something . . . something that happened somewhere before."

"You are. The last time you were here with Cal." They both laughed.

"No. It's not that, Michael. It's a feeling of déjà vu, a feeling of . . . or a longing for . . . something. It's almost a homesickness. Have you never had that experience?"

"I don't think so. On those occasions that I've looked at the stars, like tonight, I've marvelled at the majesty of the heavens. But I've never been homesick to go there."

Laughing at herself as much as at Michael's comment, Laurel said, "Tell me about your mission."

"It was the most marvelous experience of my life. I learned more about myself and about the love of God than I can ever express."

"How was your health?"

"For the most part it was okay. On one occasion I . . . they had to put me in the hospital. It was pretty bad for awhile—then my companion and my mission president gave me a blessing and everything cleared up."

"It sounds as though you got close to your mission president."

"I did. He and his wife helped all the missionaries understand how they could work to their full potential. More than that, though, the missionaries could feel of their love. It was a tangible thing. Toward the end of my mission I worked in the mission office, and President Nixon and I got really close."

"In what way?"

"Just before I was released he gave me some advice, and I told him of some of my goals."

"What were your goals, and what was his advice?"

"Oh, they're not anything spectacular."

"Tell me about them."

"We talked about marriage, children, and other things."

"Go on."

Pausing while he gathered his courage, Michael debated with himself about telling Laurel what his thoughts on marriage were. If she only knew the truth . . . but that could never be. Perhaps he could tell her some of what he and the mission president talked about. After all, she was engaged, so it would not be as though he were talking about her.

"I told President Nixon that I was a little frightened about what comes next after my mission. Especially marriage—I told him I didn't want to make a mistake."

"What did he say?"

Michael laughed, "I still remember his words. He said: 'If you continue to live the principles of the gospel, and stay clean in mind and body, you'll find some sweet innocent girl, and she'll need your love and attention. You'll love her as you love your own flesh, and you'll want to do all in your power to protect her and make her happy.'"

Laurel was silent, so Michael continued: "One of my fears was that I wouldn't know who was the right person for me to marry. I told him that I wanted my home to be forever, with us as one, and . . ." Michael paused and laughed in embarrassment.

"Please continue."

"It's just . . . I've always thought of home as a fireside. A family isn't a family until they're sitting by a fire. Does that seem silly?"

"Not at all." Laurel seemed unusually quiet as she softly asked, "What did your mission president say next?"

"He said that when I found the right girl it would be worth everything to me. Then he quoted from Proverbs, 'Who can find a virtuous woman? for her price is far above rubies.'"

"Did he say anything else?"

"Not much. We knelt in prayer and he specifically asked the Lord to help me find the right person to marry."

They sat for a long period looking at the stars and saying nothing. Finally, without a word, Laurel started the car and drove Michael to his sister's house. Puzzling over her actions, Michael wondered what he'd done wrong. Then she surprised him by saying, "Could we meet and talk again tomorrow at the same time?"

"Let's see. There's a midterm Monday that I should study for, and . . ."

"Please, Michael. It's important."

"Sure. Let's meet at the Wilkinson Center again. That way I can keep studying until you get there."

"See you tomorrow. And Michael—thanks."

Trying to get to sleep that night was again difficult. Michael kept thinking of Laurel and their meeting. *What did Laurel mean when she thanked him? And what was so important about meeting again tomorrow night?*

What about his longer term goals of marriage and a family? How was he going to find the right girl when he kept being diverted by Laurel—an engaged woman? But why did he feel about her as he did? After their meeting tomorrow he'd have to put her out of his mind and get on with his life. Why was everything in life so difficult? . . .

Sleeping completely through the night was a refreshing change for Michael, probably due to his complete exhaustion. He was more alert than he'd recently been in his morning classes, and he managed to concentrate on the subject matter. In the afternoon, however, his studies didn't go so well. Thinking about Laurel and their upcoming meeting conflicted with his need to prepare for the Monday midterm in chemistry.

Catching a brief dinner in the cafeteria, Michael continued with his studies. Finally, promptly at nine o'clock, Laurel walked up and peered over his shoulder. Looking at his chemical formulas, she wrinkled her nose. "That looks horrible. How can you make sense of it?"

"Unfortunately, sometimes I don't," Michael said with a wry grin.

"Shall we go?" she asked anxiously.

"Sure. Where this time?"

"Let's go back where we went last night. I like it up on the mountain."

"Okay, if you've got a car."

"Cal loaned me his convertible again."

"Doesn't he object to your using it for this purpose?"

Smiling, partly to herself, Laurel said: "He did ask a few more questions this time. He was kind, though, and he let me take it."

Arriving at the plateau high in Rock Canyon where they'd been the previous night, Laurel seemed anxious about something. She didn't let the convertible top down.

"Michael, did I ever tell you about my patriarchal blessing?"

"I don't think so. Why?"

"Would you like to read it?"

Surprised at Laurel's strange request, Michael wondered what it meant. Why would Laurel want him to read her patriarchal blessing? The privilege of reading such blessings was usually reserved for close family members or others the individuals felt close to. What was going on?

Concealing his surprise, Michael said, "Sure, I'd like to read it."

Fumbling with her purse, Michael was astonished to see Laurel's hands shaking. Taking out some folded papers, Laurel handed them to Michael and turned on the reading light.

Beginning to read, he saw that the blessing began in much the same way as other patriarchal blessings he'd read. But as his eyes moved along, certain words suddenly flashed an astonishing message to his startled eyes. He could hardly read fast enough to assimilate what his brain was telling him. The pertinent words were:

. . . *and dear sister, the time will come when you will yearn for companionship. It is the Lord's will that you should have a companion for life from among the noble sons of Adam.*

By these tokens you will know the one whom the Lord would approve. He will be a bearer of the Holy Priesthood, be clean of body and mind, love you as he loves his own flesh, and do all things in his power to protect you and make you happy. During the period of courtship a sweet love will grow between you and the one of your choice, and he will be inclined, as you should be, to go to the holy temple and there, over the altar of marriage, be united for time and all eternity.

It is the Lord's will that you should have a home and a fireside, and children around that fireside, with the prattle of childhood and the songs and gaiety of youth, joy and peace characterizing the setting. Set your heart on this great achievement.

Do not be distracted by the glamour of the world, for that glamour is but a dull glow in comparison to the shining light of truth that awaits you if you are true to your potential. You were chosen before this world for a special mission. . . .

Sitting in stunned silence, Michael reread portions of the blessing, as if he couldn't believe what he'd first read. He looked at Laurel and saw that she was crying. Wiping her eyes, she said: "What do you think?"

"It's amazing. I've heard of things like that, but . . ."

"Did you notice the words, 'he would love me as he loves his own flesh, and do all things to protect me and make me happy'? Those were the same words you used as you discussed what you and your mission president talked about."

"How could I forget?"

"You also commented that you wanted a fireside with your family sitting around the fire. Do you remember?"

"Yes. There's another thing about your blessing, though, that I didn't talk about."

"What?" Laurel asked with her lip quivering.

"When I was a baby and they first discovered that I had cystic fibrosis I almost died. My father gave me a blessing and my mother recorded most of it. He promised me that I would live to serve a mission, marry, and have children. Then he said that I had been . . ." Michael struggled to bring his emotions under control, and then he continued. "He said that I had been chosen for a unique mission. It was similar to what you were told in your patriarchal blessing."

Sobbing softly, Laurel leaned her head on Michael's shoulder. He reached for her hand with one hand and fumbled for a tissue with the other. Laurel dabbed at her eyes and they sat in a silent embrace for a long moment. Both of them were stunned by the astonishing and wondrous events of the moment. Suddenly, it seemed that their spirits were acknowledging each other from—from a distant sphere. There was an awakened knowledge of a former time and place . . . of a love known before.

Recovering somewhat from her shock, Laurel asked, "What shall we do?"

Mustering all the wisdom he could for the occasion, Michael muttered, "I don't know," and they both laughed through their tears.

"Maybe we could start by getting reacquainted with each other," Michael said. "I've changed since my mission, and so have you."

"That's a good idea, Michael. And I suppose I should . . . I should say something to Cal."

"Yes, you should. The trouble is, we may have to start walking everywhere we go. This convertible is great." They both chuckled and Laurel commented: "Dad has an old car that he says I can use if I want. As long as I was dating Cal I didn't need it, but now, things are different."

"What're you going to tell Cal?"

"I'm not sure. Probably I'll tell him that we should put our marriage plans on hold for a while."

"That's a *good* idea," Michael said with emphasis.

Laughing, Laurel asked, "But what about us?"

"What do you mean?"

"You said that we should get reacquainted. How do you feel about me, though?"

Michael became suddenly serious. "Laurel, I . . . how can I say it? Since that summer when I was staying with Aunt Lori, and we spent so much time together, I've loved you. Everything about you is wonderful to me. When I got your letter on my mission, the one about Cal, it nearly destroyed me."

Looking surprised, Laurel asked, "Why did you never say anything—even in your letters?"

"Because I never figured . . . you always seemed so out of reach. How could I compete against those other guys like Cal?

You're such a beautiful creature Laurel, and I . . . well you see what I am. What chance would I have?"

"Why Michael, you're one of the most sensitive, thoughtful men I know. That was what attracted me to you that summer. You had such wonderful ideas about the future."

"You were attracted to me?" Michael asked with incredulity.

"Of course I was. Why do you suppose I kept coming over to the Blairs' house?"

"I thought it was for the horses."

Laughing, as she thought back, Laurel said, "Of course I liked the horses, but we've got horses too."

"Then, Laurel, do you think you could ever . . . that is, could you ever . . .?"

Smiling, Laurel leaned close to Michael. His beating heart was pounding so hard he was sure she heard it. Drawing close, he gazed into those lovely blue eyes, the laughing eyes that now were closing, and . . . and they kissed in an embrace that spoke of love—a love that antedated any memory that either of them had, an eternal legacy of love—they were lost to everything but themselves. The future and its problems seemed insignificant in the ecstasy of the magnificent present.

Epilogue

The following article appeared in a recent edition of the "Oakland Tribune," in the society section.

Labor Day Success for
Cystic Fibrosis Foundation

Mrs. Barbara Blair, the wife of Professor John Blair of the University of California, successfully sponsored another fund-raising event for the Cystic Fibrosis Foundation. A benefit concert was held at the University of California Zellerbach Hall featuring the Berkeley Symphony Orchestra and the guest piano soloist, John Blair, Jr., the son of Professor and Mrs. Blair. Mr. Blair, Jr. played Rachmaninoff's Piano Concerto No. 3 and Prokofiev's Piano Concert No. 3., and he received a standing ovation for both pieces.

The evening was dedicated to cystic fibrosis victims, with particular recognition of a nephew of Professor Blair's, Mr. Michael Blair, who is currently studying engineering at Brigham Young University in Utah. Mr. Blair was recently married in the Salt Lake Temple of The Church of Jesus Christ of Latter-day Saints to the former Laurel Pratt.

Several other cystic fibrosis patients attended the concert. Mr. Michael Blair acted as spokesperson on behalf of those with the disease who were present. He said that although cystic fibrosis could be a debilitating disease, it need not prohibit those who had it from enjoying the rich benefits of life, including marriage, work, and having children. To dramatically demonstrate his own dedication to a full life, he invited his lovely wife to the stand.

Laurel Pratt Blair, who was stunning with her green chiffon dress and flaming red hair, entered into the festivities of the evening by bounding to the stage and embracing her husband. She told the audience, with a twinkle in her eye,

193

that her marriage to Michael Blair had been arranged in heaven. The audience loved it.

Present at the concert were several dignitaries from Berkeley and the University of California. Chancellor Chang-Lin Tien was present as was President Jack Peltason of the University of California. Both officials stated how much they enjoyed the evening. Loni Hancock, the mayor of Berkeley, was also present.

The Blairs have numerous relatives who live in Utah, and some of them came to Berkeley for the event. After the concert an open house was held in the spacious home of Professor and Barbara Blair, and many of their relatives were there. Among those from Utah were Lori Blair, her daughter Ruth Blair, and her son Jeff who was recently appointed Associate Professor of Philosophy at the University of California. Lori Blair helped with the fund raising for the event, particularly in Utah. Alma and Janis Pratt, the father and mother of Laurel Blair, were also in attendance.

As is usual with an event that Barbara Blair sponsors, the entire evening was a resounding success. A check for more than $50,000 was presented to a representative of the Cystic Fibrosis Foundation.

In memory of Martha Blair, the mother of Professor John Blair, a poem was read by her granddaughter, Lucinda Blair. Lucinda, the daughter of Barbara and Professor John Blair, is a talented young lady currently attending the University of California. The poem was her own composition and it sensitively testified to the greatness of the lady who was the mother and grandmother of many of those present.

This demonstrates again what we can do in Berkeley and Oakland if we just have the will to do it. This reporter offers congratulations to Barbara Blair and all those who participated in creating a marvelous evening.

Selected Bibliography

Latter-day Saint Scriptures

The Book of Mormon—Another Testament of Jesus Christ. Translated by Joseph Smith, Junior. Salt Lake City, Utah: The Church of Jesus Christ of Latter-day Saints, 1989.

The Doctrine and Covenants of The Church of Jesus Christ of Latter-day Saints. Salt Lake City, Utah: The Church of Jesus Christ of Latter-day Saints, 1989.

The Holy Bible. Authorized King James Version. Salt Lake City, Utah: Published by The Church of Jesus Christ of Latter-day Saints, 1979.

The Pearl of Great Price. Salt Lake City, Utah: The Church of Jesus Christ of Latter-day Saints, 1989.

Latter-day Saint Historical and Doctrinal Books and CDs

Encyclopedia of Mormonism, "The History, Scripture, Doctrine, and Procedure of the Church of Jesus Christ of Latter-day Saints." Edited by Daniel H. Ludlow, 4 volumes. New York, N.Y.: Macmillan Publishing Company, 1992.

Gospel Library—Third Edition. CD ROM, Orem, Utah: Infobases International Inc., 1993.

History of the Church of Jesus Christ of Latter-day Saints, 7 volumes plus Index. Salt Lake City, Utah: Deseret Book Company, 1970.

Journal of Discourses, 26 volumes. Los Angeles, CA: General Printing and Lithograph Co., 1961.

LDS Historical Library—Second Edition. CD ROM, Orem, Utah: Infobases International Inc., 1993.

Madsen, Truman G., *Eternal Man.* Salt Lake City, Utah: Deseret Book Company, 1966.

McConkie, Bruce R., *Mormon Doctrine.* Salt Lake City, Utah: Bookcraft, Inc., 1958.

Smith, Joseph Fielding, "Gospel Doctrine," *Gospel Library, Third Edition.* Provo, Utah: Computer CD from Folio Infobase, 1993.

Talmage, James E., *Jesus the Christ.* Salt Lake City, Utah: Deseret Book Company, 1982.

Teachings of the Prophet Joseph Smith. Compiled by Joseph Fielding Smith. Salt Lake City, Utah: The Church of Jesus Christ of Latter-day Saints, 1938.

Young, Brigham, *Discourses of Brigham Young.* Edited by John A. Widtsoe, Salt Lake City, Utah: Deseret Book Company, 1946.

Near-Death Literature

Almeder, Robert, *Beyond Death.* Springfield, Illinois: Publisher, Charles C. Thomas, 1987.

Atwater, P.M.H., *Coming Back to Life.* New York, N.Y.: Ballantine Books, 1988.

Atwater, P.M.H., "Is There A Hell? Surprising Observations About the Near-Death Experience." *Journal of Near-Death Studies*, Vol. 10, No. 3, Spring 1992. New York, N.Y.: Human Sciences Press.

Brinkley, Dannion, with Perry, Paul, *Saved by the Light—The True Story of a Man Who Died Twice and the Profound Revelations He Received.* New York, N.Y.: Villard Books, 1994.

Christensen, Kevin, "Nigh unto Death: NDE Research and the Book of Mormon." *Journal of Book of Mormon Studies*, Vol 2, No. 1, Spring 1993. Provo, Utah: Foundation for Ancient Research & Mormon Studies.

Crowther, Duane S., *Life Everlasting.* Salt Lake City, Utah: Bookcraft, Inc., 1967.

Eadie, Betty J., *Embraced by the Light.* Placerville, California: Gold Leaf Press, 1992.

Flynn, Charles P., *After the Beyond—Human Transformation and the Near-Death Experience.* New York, N.Y.: Prentice Hall Press, 1986.

Gallup, G., Jr., *Adventures in Immortality.* New York, N.Y.: McGraw Hill, 1982.

Gibson, Arvin S., *Glimpses of Eternity.* Bountiful, Utah: Horizon Publishers and Distributors, Inc., 1992.

Gibson, Arvin S., *Echoes From Eternity.* Bountiful, Utah: Horizon Publishers and Distributors, Inc., 1993.

Gibson, Arvin S., *Journeys Beyond Life.* Bountiful, Utah: Horizon Publishers and Distributors, Inc., 1994.

Grey, Margot, *Return from Death.* London, England and New York, N.Y.: Arkana, 1987.

Grosso, Michael, *The Final Choice*. Walpose, New Hampshire: Stillpoint Publishing, 1985.

Harris, Barbara, and Bascom, Lionel C., *Full Circle*. New York, N.Y.: Pocket Books, 1990.

Kübler-Ross, Elisabeth, *On Children and Death*. New York, N.Y.: Collier Books, MacMillan Publishing Company, 1983.

Kübler-Ross, Elisabeth, *Questions and Answers on Death and Dying*. New York, N.Y: Collier Books, MacMillan Publishing Company, 1974.

Lundahl, Craig R., *A Collection of Near-Death Research Readings*. Chicago, Ill.: Nelson-Hall Publishers, 1982.

Millett, Larry R., *A Touch of Here and Beyond*. Salt Lake City, Utah: Hawkes Publishing, Inc.

Moody, Raymond A., Jr., *Life After Life*. New York, N.Y.: Bantam Books, 1988.

Moody, Raymond A., Jr., *The Light Beyond*. Bantam Books, New York, N.Y., 1988.

Moody, Raymond A. Jr., M.D., *Reflections on Life After Life*, New York, N.Y.: Bantam Books, 1983.

Morse, Melvin with Perry, Paul, *Closer to the Light*. New York, N.Y.: Villard Books, 1990.

Morse, Melvin with Perry, Paul, *Transformed by the Light*. New York, N.Y.: Villard Books, 1992.

Murphet, Howard, *Beyond Death*. Wheaton, Illinois: Quest Books, The Theosophical Publishing House, 1990.

Nelson, Lee, *Beyond the Veil—Volume I*. Orem, Utah: Cedar Fort Inc., 1988.

Nelson, Lee, *Beyond the Veil—Volume II*. Orem, Utah: Cedar Fort Inc., 1989.

Rawlings, Maurice, *Beyond Death's Door*. New York, N.Y.: Bantam Books, 1979.

Rawlings, Maurice, *To Hell and Back*. Nashville, Tennessee: Thomas Nelson Publishers, 1993.

Ring, Kenneth, *Heading Toward Omega*. New York, N. Y.: William Morrow Inc.,1985.

Ring, Kenneth, *Life at Death*. New York, N.Y.: Quill, 1982.

Ritchie, George G. with Sherrill, Elizabeth, *Return from Tomorrow*. Old Tappan, New Jersey: Spire Books, Fleming H. Revell Co., 1978.

Ritchie, George G., *My Life After Dying—Becoming Alive to Universal Love.* Norfolk, Virginia: Hampton Roads Publishing, 1991.

Sorensen, Michele R.; Willmore, David R., *The Journey Beyond Life, Vol. One.* Orem, Utah: Family Affair Books, 1988.

Storm, Howard, unpublished document in possession of author; transcribed from taped experience recorded in 1989 at The NDE Research Institute, Fort Thomas, Kentucky.

Top, Brent L. and Wendy C., *Beyond Death's Door—Understanding Near-Death Experiences in Light of the Restored Gospel.* Salt Lake City, Utah: Bookcraft, 1993.

Wallace, Ranelle, with Taylor, Curtis, *The Burning Within.* Carson City, Nevada: Gold Leaf Press, 1994.

Wilson, Ian, *The After Death Experience.* New York, N.Y.: William Morrow and Company, Inc., 1987.

Wren-Lewis, John, "Avoiding the Columbus Confusion: An Ockhamish View of Near-Death Research," *Journal of Near-Death Studies*, Vol. 11, No. 2, Winter 1992. 233 Spring St., New York, N.Y.: Human Sciences Press, Inc.,

Zaleski, Carol. *Otherworld Journeys.* New York, N.Y. and Oxford, England: Oxford University Press, 1987.

Other Literature

Davies, Paul, *The Mind of God—The Scientific Basis for a Rational World.* New York, N.Y.: Simon and Schuster, 1992.

Diamond, Jared, *The Third Chimpanzee—The Evolution and Future of the Human Animal.* New York, N.Y.: Harper Collins, 1992.

Du Noüy, Lecomte, *Human Destiny.* New York, N.Y., London, England: Longmans, Green and Co., 1947.

Gibson, Arvin S., *In Search of Angels.* Bountiful, Utah: Horizon Publishers and Distributors, Inc., 1990.

Gregory, Richard L., *The Oxford Companion to the Mind.* Oxford, England, New York, N.Y.: Oxford University Press, 1987.

Hawking, Stephen W., *A Brief History of Time—From the Big Bang to Black Holes.* New York, N.Y., London, England: Bantam Books, 1988.

Johnson, Phillip E., *Darwin on Trial.* Washington, D.C.: Regnery Gateway, 1991.

Lindley, David, *The End of Physics—The Myth of a Unified Theory*. New York, N.Y.: Basic Books, Harper Collins, 1993.

Salisbury, Frank B., *The Creation*. Salt Lake City, Utah: Deseret Book Company, 1976.

Schroeder, Gerald L., *Genesis and the Big Bang—The Discovery of Harmony Between Modern Science and the Bible*. New York, N.Y., London, England: Bantam Books, 1992.

Schwartz, Jeffrey H., *What the Bones Tell Us—An Anthropologist Examines the Evidence in an Attempt to Unravel Ancient Mysteries and Modern Crimes*. New York, N.Y.: Henry Holt and Co., 1993.

Spanos, Nicholas P.; Menary, Evelyn; Gabora, Natalie DuBreuil, Susan C.; and Dewhirst, Bridget; "Secondary Identity Enactments During Hypnotic Past-Life Regression: A Sociocognitive Perspective;" *Journal of Personality and Social Psychology*, 1991, Vol. 61, No. 2.

White, Michael and Gribbin, John, *Stephen Hawking—A Life in Science*. New York, N.Y.: A Dutton Book, 1992.